JENNIFER WEST
Sometimes a Miracle

Silhouette Special Edition

Published by Silhouette Books New York

America's Publisher of Contemporary Romance

To my friends, the sushi chefs at Restaurant Taiko.
You give me a place where ideas grow easily
in the warmth of your smiles. Thank you for many
happy times, Onogawa-san, Suzuki-san,
Ko-Chan-san, Arai-san, and Kinoki-san.

SILHOUETTE BOOKS
300 East 42nd St., New York, N.Y. 10017

Copyright © 1987 by Jennifer West

ISBN: 0-373-09404-3

First Silhouette Books printing September 1987

America's Publisher of Contemporary Romance

Printed in the U.S.A.

"What's wrong with loving me?"

Alex had to have the answer.

"You aren't the man I wanted, Alex," Cassandra whispered. "I wanted a man who could provide some substance and security to our existence. I used to dream of a man who would sweep me off my feet, protect me from the..."

Tears were streaming down her face. She was trying to fight her own devils and not doing a very good job of it.

Alex wanted to go to her, to slay each and every dragon at her doorstep, but he couldn't. She had to invite him in. She had to, and she had to do it now, or it was never going to happen....

Dear Reader,

Spellbinders! That's what we're striving for. The editors at Silhouette are determined to capture your imagination and win your heart with every single book we publish. Each month, six Special Editions are chosen with *you* in mind.

Our authors are our inspiration. Writers such as Nora Roberts, Tracy Sinclair, Kathleen Eagle, Carole Halston and Linda Howard—to name but a few—are masters at creating endearing characters and heartrending love stories. Their characters are everyday people—just like you and me—whose lives have been touched by love, whose dreams and desires suddenly come true!

So find a cozy, quiet place to read, and create your own special moment with a Silhouette Special Edition.

Sincerely,

The Editors
SILHOUETTE BOOKS

dr

Books by Jennifer West

Silhouette Intimate Moments

A Season of Rainbows #10
Star Spangled Days #31
Edge of Venus #71
Main Chance #99

Silhouette Special Edition

Earth and Fire #262
Return to Paradise #283
Moments of Glory #339
Object of Desire #366
Come Pride, Come Passion #383
Sometimes a Miracle #404

JENNIFER WEST

was born into a family of concert artists and mad inventors in Brooklyn, New York. After her studies in the dramatic arts, she enjoyed a career in musical comedy. Her current hobby is tracing her roots to see if she has claim to any European throne. In the meantime she writes novels, television scripts and short stories. Jennifer's husband, son, two Akita dogs and an indeterminate number of goldfish share a busy residence in Irvine, California.

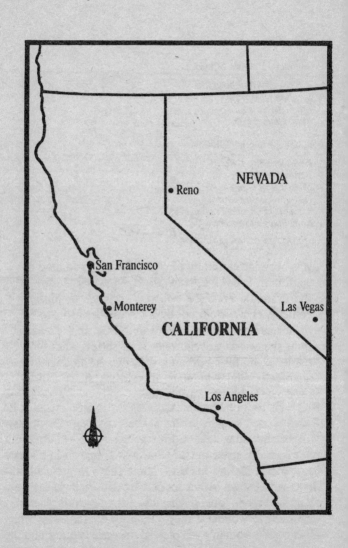

Chapter One

There was a time when Alex Montana—known during his more infamous days as rodeo star Rocky Montana—would have died before he would have gone to anyone for help in fighting a battle. Specifically that time would have been before he fell off a crazy black Brahma bull, got his ribs kicked in, his guts squashed out, and his right shoulder permanently rearranged. So, as he stared across the street at the Santa Monica, California storefront sign reading Kenzo School of Martial Arts and Protection Agency, he found himself swallowing hard. Pride didn't go down easy.

A minute later he stood inside the same building and tried to make sense out of what was going on in a single large room. Before his eyes, some thirty white-clad students with brown sashes looped around their waists were standing on one foot, staring at a mirrored wall. Alex was beginning to wonder if they might not die that way, when all at once a woman's yell pierced the eerie stillness and the mesmerized human storks went into violent action with their arms and legs flaying about in various directions. If air could die, it had just been slain. And then it was over. The strange group dispersed in sections of twos and threes, everyone talking like normal people.

The woman who had yelled and dismantled the group moved rapidly across the room. Her hair was barely shoulder length and was a bright honeyed shade, streaked with even lighter tones that looked as though they might even be natural. It appeared too thick for the black clasp she had attempted to bind it in. Even as Alex thought this, she reached back and released the straining locks from bondage, then with unself-conscious abandon, shook her mane free. He continued to watch her with appreciation. Interesting walk, he thought; nice swing to it. And the rest of her, from what he could make out, wasn't bad, either. She disappeared behind a door before he could do a thorough analysis.

For another moment, Alex stood in place, trying to get a fix on where he was to go. He had expected an office in a building: something akin to what was shown on television when someone went to a detective agency. He looked again at the card in his hand. It read Kenzo Protection Agency, all right, and the sign outside agreed. There was nothing on the card about the school, however.

Across the room he heard what sounded like a drawer being forcefully slammed. There was another furious wham, then some muttering. The noises came from behind the door. On it, in stick-on gold letters, was the word Office—he hadn't noticed that before—then below, Kenzo Protection Agency, and beneath that plaque of little distinction was Ogata Kenzo's name.

Alex crossed the room and rapped against the wood. It wasn't actually wood, however. It was a photographed veneer of mahogany on particle board, sandwiched over a hollow center. The *i* in Office came loose and fluttered to the floor. He picked it up and had it in his hand when he entered upon the words "Yes! All right!" issuing from within.

"What can I do for you?" said the woman seated behind the desk opposite him. The "you" had been emphasized, as if he were part of a long line of others. She was eyeing him warily, with an expression of defeated weariness. Still, if he were rating faces, hers would be up there with the best of them.

"Well . . ." he said, and was about to launch into one of the usual lines he'd throw out to a question such as "What can I do for you?," when posed by a beautiful woman. But he didn't. "I'm here to see Mr. Kenzo," he said instead, deciding to get on with the more serious business.

The thing of it was, he didn't actually have all that much time these days to fool around; unless, of course, he could be certain he was onto a sure thing. In that case, he could see his way clear to making an allowance to expand his schedule. But this one, with her tiredness and suspicious vibes, didn't look to be that easy a conquest.

"Actually," she answered worriedly, "that's not really possible—to see him."

"How's that?" Alex returned, starting to worry himself.

Her face grew very white, as if she had just been given some bad news. Alex began to feel even more uneasy. Perhaps she looked so wan because she was about to dispense bad tidings to *him*. Being on the receiving end of disastrous news bulletins had lately become a steady thing in his life.

Shifting uncomfortably in her chair, she seemed about to end the suspense when the telephone rang, at which point she launched into a cryptic conversation with the caller. Delays of any kind always made Alex uneasy: a snag forebode more snags, and enough snags foretold all-out failure. Maybe, he told himself, he was just prone to pessimism lately.

Drawing his mind away from his fears, he instead concentrated on the conversation underway. That was a waste of time, though. There was no way to make sense out of her end of the dialogue. She answered in brief sighs, a "yes" here, a "no" there, a "possibly" and several insecure "maybes."

It was also impossible to get a fix on the situation by mere observation. The only thing he would lay money on was that it wasn't her jolliest moment. Her face had become a shifting canvas of expressions, registering emotions that ranged from sympathetic to weary to defensive, to just plain stunned. And all the while, Alex was finding it increasingly difficult not to admire the rest of her; she certainly was a good-looking female. Again his thoughts drifted to what tack he might employ to corral her into his stable for the night.

Then he remembered how he might not have all that many nights left to play Romeo. Considerately, Doom had slipped a cold bony hand on his shoulder. It was a reminder: he wasn't a man who could just throw nights away anymore, as if scattering birdseed to the wind. No, indeed. Time was now a commodity to be cherished, not squandered lightly on every pretty passing face and appealing body. Discrimination was the current watchword. Think of yourself as a human hourglass, lad, the sands of time sifting out from your body with each exhalation.

Such was his situation.

Yet he still had a dash of the old reckless buckaroo left in him, and he examined the woman more intently, trying to make a case for going the way of his libido. Wonderful eyes, really great eyes. Yeah, he thought, buoyed by his favorable assessment, she would be worth a night—or two or three, even. Still, he considered more dispassionately, she didn't look all that easy; not enough to warrant an investment of his energies, anyway, where there was little chance of a reasonable payoff.

He withdrew his eyes from the blonde, regrouping his thoughts on the actual purpose of his visit as he took in the rest of his surroundings.

The room he found himself in was small. Ten of his steps would have covered the entire territory; a large horse would have been crowded. The walls were yellow but were meant to be white. The desk had a wad of paper beneath one leg to keep it from wobbling. There were two chairs of equal levels of disrepute scrunched between him and the desk. On the dingy walls were some movie posters of Bruce Lee, a few photographs of another man in white pajamas leaping into the air, feet and arms extended in what Alex considered an impossible display of physical contortion, and an assemblage of official-looking diplomas stacked one below the other in a neat vertical line.

The conversation ended. She replaced the telephone and looked up. "Sorry," she said.

"No problem." He sat up and recrossed his legs, preliminary steps to getting down to his own business once again. "Mr. Kenzo," Alex said, reintroducing the topic of his own dialogue with her. "The reason I'm here. I need to see him right away."

"Yes," she said with a faint sigh. Moving her attention to a corner of the ceiling, she said, "But you see, Og's not here. So no one can see him. Not me, not you, not anyone."

"Og?"

"Ogata," the woman explained, her glance returning to him. "Ogata Kenzo. I'm sorry, but he's not here. I don't know when he'll be back."

"We had an appointment," Alex informed, as if that fact would make the difference. "I wrote. He answered."

"But he's still not here." She offered nothing more, only the continuing expression of mild despair.

They stared at each other. The woman was also wearing one of the white pajama outfits. Her hair was as shiny as silk underwear, Alex thought, which led him to think further along the same lines. She had a good body, possibly a great one, from what he could see of it, lost as it was in the white pajama affair. Her eyes were amazingly blue, and with a certain twinge of nostalgia, he thought of the wide skies of Montana where he had been raised. The nose was plain and sensible. To someone given to more sociological or anatomical analysis, he supposed its shape might signify a certain degree of elevated class. As for the mouth, it was full and probably as pretty as any he had kissed during his more successful bronco-busting days, except that at the moment it was drawn into a stern line.

"Alex Montana—that's who I am. Now then," he rushed on, "the thing of it is, I have a contract with Mr. Kenzo, or whatever his name is. A contract," Alex repeated, "as in money—a lot of it—crossing palms. The agreement was that Mr. Kenzo was going to be here when I needed him. I'm here, and I need him."

The woman bit her lower lip this time, and her eyes skittered off, losing their focus as she sought information in the cosmos. "Rocky Montana?" she said uncertainly, looking at him again, but with more recognition.

That Alex found heartening. He nodded. "The Rocky days are over, though. Just plain Alex will do."

"Look, I'm sorry," she said, appearing both annoyed and embarrassed that he was there to collect on his part of the agreement. "Og had a lot of deals going that I didn't know about. I only heard him mention your name once in passing. So there's still nothing I can do to help you."

Again he might have said something slyly provocative. But now he kept to the topic at hand, which was the matter of keeping himself alive over the next fifteen days.

"I realize that," he said instead, politely. It was difficult not to lose his patience. After all, he was a man who could lose his life. It wasn't as if someone had misplaced a receipt or something and they'd call him when they found it. He might not be around to pick up the phone. "And that's why I'm here to see your boss," Alex continued with the strained patience of a saint dangerously on the edge of being decanonized.

"Partner," she corrected immediately. "Og's my partner. Unfortunately," she muttered. Her fingers idly flipped through a stack of unopened envelopes. Alex noted several were stamped Open Immediately in screaming red ink.

"Partner," he amended, because he felt it might be important to her, since she had made it such an issue. "I'd appreciate it if you could put me through to your partner, then."

She stood. Her every movement was remarkably graceful and feminine and unified. Alex guessed she was five-six, not tall, not short, a pleasing height for a woman. He noted that her wrists sticking from the white cloth sleeves were incredibly fragile.

Looking down at him in the chair, she said, "The thing of it is, Og's gone. I get the feeling you don't understand me. Or believe me. Whatever. Og's really gone. As in blown town. As in split. Actually, I don't know where he is and I don't know when, or if, he'll ever be back."

"I see." The speech put a whole new complexion on the matter. Alex considered his options. "And what about our money?"

"There isn't any." She sighed sadly, as if it were she who were out of pocket. "That's why Og took off."

"Oh." He considered this as valid, then, just for the hell of it, said, "I could sue."

She nodded sagely. "Sure, why not? Everyone else is."

"But I wouldn't get anything."

"A headache maybe."

"So," Alex said, casting about in a lake he already sensed had no fish, "what about the protection my associates and I paid for?"

"Here's looking at you, kid."

"Uh-huh. Yup." He stared at her for a long moment. "So you're all I've got, huh?"

She pressed her lips together and shook her head sorrowfully. "All you've got. Take it or leave it," she said with a shrug. Then with more animation, she added, "Anyway, for what it's worth to you, I'm tougher than I look. I was his best student. Og taught me a lot. He just didn't teach me about him," she finished ruefully.

"Well, sounds like ol' Og was just a hell of a guy," Alex said. "When he was here."

She winced. "When he was here...." She was half sitting, half leaning on the corner of the desk, which had tilted slightly in spite of the wad of paper shoring up the leg. "Look, if it's because I'm a woman, believe me, my feelings aren't hurt. I've better things to do at the moment than carry a placard for women's rights. Is it?" she asked suddenly.

"Is it what?"

"Is it because I'm a woman? You're afraid I can't do the job because I'm a woman?"

"Yeah. Yeah, of course it's because you're a woman. No offense intended, but your chicken wrists don't exactly inspire a whole lot of confidence. I don't mean to undermine your sense of self-worth, or anything—you might bake a mean apple pie. But I'm looking to save my skin, here. Bottom line is, did he teach you how to stop killers?"

She considered the question. "Theoretically."

"Theoretically?" Alex stared at her, incredulous. "Oh, yeah, sure. I get it. You stop them by discussing the situation. A guy comes forth with a .45 caliber and you sit down with him and reason the problem out."

"No," she replied, somewhat offended. "I mean, I haven't had any direct hands-on experience. If that's what you were getting at."

"I was. Exactly. My money wasn't meant to go for theories."

"Look, Mr. Montana," she said miserably, "the fact is, I'm really sorry about your money. Honestly. And if it makes you feel any better, a lot of people—including yours truly—are in the same lousy place."

"Well, thanks. Nice of you to cheer me up. Only it doesn't. I'm not filled with gladness or relief, and you can scratch compassion clear off the board. Somehow my imminent disappearance off the face of the earth has dulled my concern over the financial plights of others."

"They're *really* out to get you?"

He stared at her. "Yes. They are really out to get me." He smiled ruefully. "And I don't think it's going to be a hell of a hard thing to pick me off now, either. So, as they say, gotta run."

He uncrossed his legs and planted both boots on the floor with a pronounced thud. Lifting himself out of the chair seemed to take forever. Okay, he was tall, but not that tall. The truth was, he was weary—bone weary. Just dragging his six-foot-two frame around was an exhausting enterprise lately. Never, when he was riding broncos, had he ever thought a man of thirty-two could fall apart so fast. He shifted his leather sports jacket so that it hung smoothly over his frame. The jeans, which had ridden up, fell easily back over the tops of his boots. Beneath the denim only a flash of pointed alligator skin toes showed, and a glimpse of heels. They were his dress boots, and the jacket represented his best effort at city dressing.

"If there was anything I could do—"

"Hey," Alex said, "don't sweat it. Easy come, easy go. But if you read about me in the papers, find out where the wake'll be held. You can bake a pie for it. You owe me," he said, and saluted her before turning. He covered the three feet it took to reach the door and was about to step through when Ogata Kenzo's partner spoke.

"Mr. Montana—"

Alex turned.

"You're really serious?"

"Dead serious. Unfortunately."

"Someone's out there trying to kill you? I mean, Og was always very dramatic. Everything larger than life. I tend not to believe too much anymore. But this...this problem you have...this is no kidding around?"

"Unfortunately, no. I have it on direct experience. The Grim Reaper is dogging my footsteps."

"You're *sure*?"

She seemed not to want to believe him. He did not want to believe it, either. But there it was.

"Positive," he said.

"How are you sure?" she asked, coming around the desk with an expression of genuine concern.

"I got hit over the head two weeks ago when I entered my apartment, and someone tried to run me over last week. I took both incidents as clues that someone didn't want my presence on the planet much longer."

"Oh. Well, yeah. Probably a valid assumption." For an instant she seemed to waver between retreat and taking some sort of action. Finally she said in a voice lacking conviction, "I'm Cassandra Burke." She held out her small hand.

Alex took it, shook it lightly, amazed at how delicate it felt in his, and figured that was how she would protect him: any genuine killer would laugh himself to death the moment he got a load of what she considered her lethal weapons.

"Would you like to tell me? The whole story?" she prompted, then quickly offered a disclaimer. "Look, I don't know if it would do any good."

"It won't," he said. He couldn't help but notice again and again how pretty she was. "But it'll pass the time while I wait to be picked off." He smiled. She didn't.

"I'm a good listener," she said, seeming pleased to offer some sort of support, at last.

"Great. I'm a good talker." He slipped down into the chair again, thinking it wasn't such a bad thing, this nice view while he killed time waiting to be killed. It seemed to take him even longer to go down than it had to rise. But then, he thought, he was several minutes older already. Degeneration.

She was right. As he spun out his yarn, she proved to be an excellent audience. Encouraged by her rapt attention, he inserted dramatic embellishments, aimed to draw out sympathy wherever he felt it might serve his future purposes.

He was, Alex began, part of a consortium of failures. There were four of them: himself, being the failed cowboy; the others being a failed mobster, a failed ruthless merchant and a failed Texas oil tycoon.

As Rocky Montana he had been hell on a pony; he figured he'd been to the rodeo circuit what Mick Jagger had been to rock during his own zenith. But then there was that incident with the bull, and all was lost. For a while he went into a major emotional decline, sulking and moping for all he was worth. Eventually even he got sick of his gloomy face in the mirror. The end result was that he traded in his passion for horses for a passion for horsepower. He had always liked the feel of sitting on all that muscle power, of guiding it masterfully around the dirt arenas. So he got to work on putting together a mechanical thrill that might duplicate the rush he used to get from the horseflesh.

It took him three years of excessive, compulsive work, but he put together a new breed of engine never before seen on the planet earth. Needless to say, he didn't have a lot of development money, and that was where the other three failures came onto the scene.

He met them one by one in unlikely places.

First came Big Charlie. Charlie was corpulent and greedy and every cell of him a Texan. Once he had been considered a verifiable oil king, but that was before the world oil and gas crises in which Charlie had lost everything, right down to his wife.

"Sadly," Alex confided in Cassandra, "when I met Charlie, he had little more to his name than his pink-and-white Cadillac convertible, with a set of gigantic steer's horns on the hood."

It was this very whimsical decorative accent, Alex explained, that actually drew him and Charlie together. Charlie was out cruising away his troubles one night, while he, Alex—in a rare state of inebriation—was outside a honky-tonk cowboy bar, feeling more than sorry for himself. He stopped howling at the moon just long enough to vent his pent-up hostility on what he perceived as a pink-and-white Brahma coming at him down the middle of the road. Charlie had liked that. He said later that he thought it took a lot of style for a man to try to wrestle a Cadillac to the pavement. He liked it so well, Alex recalled with an affectionate smile, that Charlie even drove him to the hospital himself.

Then there was Gordo "the Bomb" Bombolina. It so happened, Alex related, that Gordo, like Big Charlie, was also fat. It wasn't a hereditary defect but merely gluttony caused by extreme sadness at being a failure as a mobster.

All the other boys in the old New York neighborhood had made something bad of themselves. Gordo had tried to make his bones, as he confided to Alex, but could never bring himself to carry out a single act of mayhem. The most he could make of himself was a restaurateur.

So, at Bombolina's Pizza and Spaghetti Factory, the worst of the bad boys would hold dinner meetings in between hours, knowing among themselves that they were safe in whatever they said because Gordo the Bomb was too lily-livered to squeal to anyone about what went on during those lively, murder-plotting sessions. He wasn't called the Bomb for nothing; as a mobster, he had, in fact, really bombed out.

"I met Gordo one night at his restaurant," Alex told Cassandra Burke. Nodding and smiling, seeing it all again in his mind, he painted the scene for her in words, just as it had happened.

He had come in for a plate of pasta and a couple of beers and had ended up rescuing Gordo from some young punk who'd had a feeling he could take a pizza without paying.

"In all honesty, I was truly remarkable that night," Alex said.

"Were you?" Cassandra Burke interjected with a cat's smile.

"In all humility, yes," he replied, "I was. I was magnificent in every way." He bowed his head for a beat, then, looking up, asked, "Are you going to go along with this, or—"

"Yes, yes... continue. I was just checking, you know, for the sake of absolute credibility." She waved one of her hands, gesturing for him to continue.

So he did, verbally ambling along on the same grandiose course.

He had felled the youth with one swing of his bad shoulder—which again had necessitated a trip to the hospital for realignment—and, in doing so, had earned every last cloying ounce of Gordo's admiration and gratitude for chivalrous service.

The last of the four failures to form an alliance, Alex informed her, was Jerry Friedman.

As fat as the other two were, Jerry was that thin. It came, as far as Alex could discern, from extreme nervousness and guilt. He was nervous because his jewelry store did miserably, and guilty because his wife couldn't have a new mink coat every season, a trip to the Bahamas every year, a live-in girl to save her from the drudgery of placing the dishes in the dishwasher and a phone in her Mercedes—which would make it even easier for her to complain to Jerry while en route from the tennis club to her nail appointment.

Jerry, admittedly, engineered his own downfall. He was just too kind. Whenever someone didn't have enough money for an engagement ring or a Christmas present, or whatever, Jerry reduced the prices until he, himself, could barely afford to keep his store's doors open.

"I met poor Jerry at his attorney's office. Our attorney's office." Alex paused. "Poor Jerry—that's what we always call him. You think of Jerry, you think of poor Jerry. Like ham and eggs." Alex shook his head. "Poor guy.

"Anyway, Jerry was there that day, losing the shirt off his back to Doris in their divorce settlement. I tell you, if it's ham and eggs with Jerry, mention Doris, and you think rats and the black plague. I, however, was there on a happier matter, talking patents for my engine."

It seemed right and natural, Alex said, that the four would band together to get his engine into the public's eyes. They scraped up development money to see a prototype take form. Then there were the costs for tests and trips to Detroit to see if anyone might be interested. At first blush, Detroit didn't seem to be ecstatic about an engine that might make their entire product line obsolete. But at last a ray of hope entered the picture when some corporate bureaucrat with no better sense inadvertently sent him a flyer announcing a contest featuring new and innovative automotive products to be held at the Sports Arena in Los Angeles.

Not only would the winning inventors be given enormous monetary rewards for their brilliant contribution to the industry, but the inventions would also be put into at least limited production as part of their research and design departments.

"That was two months ago," Alex said. "It seems like another lifetime."

Anticipating the contest, the spirits of the four failures rose, Alex continued. Their collective imaginations were fertile with the possibility of public exposure, and of actually winning the contest. Scenes of money and recognition danced like sugarplums in their heads. The other three partners felt that this was their last big break in life. They felt that he, Alex, was still young, and apparently brilliant, and whereas he might not ever wrestle bulls to their knees again, he could very well make it in the corporate world.

"Their overriding thought in all of this was to keep me safe."

"So that their dreams could come true."

"Exactly," Alex replied, pleased with her participation. It showed that she was caught up in the tale.

But each of them, Alex explained, had his own particular paranoia about what might happen to him and his invention.

"For one, Big Charlie felt that the oil and gas barons would rub me out rather than let me reduce their profits. My engine is vastly more economical than anything the car manufacturers are foisting on the public."

On the other hand, Alex went on, Gordo Bombolina thought the Mafia might take exception to the engine, as it would probably cut down on labor, and hence, on labor union dues, and hence, on money to skim off the top, for them.

"Jerry Friedman was the most realistic. He feared—"

"Doris."

"He did. Jerry felt Doris would rather see me six feet under than see Jerry walk in a new pair of shoes to the side of my grave."

"Especially," Cassandra joined in, "when all she'd gotten in the divorce settlement was the shirt off his back."

"Exactly," Alex said, allowing her to see that he was duly impressed. Beauty and brains and chicken wrists. Hell of a lot of potential in one woman, he conceded.

So it was therefore decided among the three, that he, Alex, would need protection for the remaining weeks before the wonder engine could be unveiled. After due consideration, they felt it would be wise to go the oriental martial arts route, as well as pack a gun. This would take care of both long-range and close-encounter attacks. But all the martial arts masters they contacted refused to use firearms. It was ignoble to their way of thinking. But the three partners weren't interested in philosophy; they were interested in money, Alex explained.

"Ha!" Cassandra commented. "They should meet Og."

"They did. At least by phone."

Ogata Kenzo was their man, straight down the line. Or so they thought. He was, as far as they could tell, Alex said, a master of martial arts, plus he was sensible. For the right amount of money, he'd carry a gun, a snake or a Hula-Hoop. It was all the same to him. The three liked his style, and sent him the check—for a sizable amount that had to be borrowed—to cover his retainer. It was understood that at the first hint of trouble, Kenzo would be on the job, protecting their human investment in the future.

"Someone," Alex said in conclusion, "definitely doesn't want me and my engine to make it to the contest."

Cassandra Burke was very still. She looked almost as if she might cry. Then she said, "That's really sad."

"Well, they haven't got me yet."

"No, I mean about those three guys with nothing to look forward to in life but—"

"But me," Alex said, slightly annoyed that she hadn't put her sympathy in his court. "Anyway," he said, rising from his seat again, "it seems that we're all going to be disappointed now, thanks to Mr. Kenzo."

"I feel terrible," Cassandra said, also rising.

"Hey, don't sweat it," Alex said. "How can there be success stories if there aren't any failures? Life wouldn't be life without death lurking out there on the horizon for contrast. We're just four guys pitching in here, doing our part."

"You're really bitter," Cassandra commented.

"Nah. I'm mad," Alex corrected sharply. "I'm ticked. Kenzo ran with our cash. And I'm probably going to be dead in a day or two. It's enough to make a man drink." He paused and looked hopefully at Cassandra. "I don't suppose you'd like to have a drink with a man destined for the bone orchard, would you?"

"No, thanks. It would be too depressing."

"You have a point."

"Why don't you hire someone else?" she asked.

"With what? Kenzo's got the last big loot any of us are going to get our hands on, until—or unless—I win that contest."

"Oh," she said despondently. Then, looking up, she asked with a note of hope, "What do you think your chances might be? To win the contest?"

"Conservatively speaking?"

"Yes."

"One hundred and fifty percent."

They spent a moment staring at each other, as if someone, or something, unseen was holding them there. He felt worlds being formed and dissolved in the blue eyes that stared him down. He felt himself dissolving. Maybe he was falling in love. Or maybe he should eat something. When had he eaten last? Life was beginning to blur lately, what with the specter of Death shuffling along behind him.

"Well," Alex said with effort, dragging himself out of the twin blue horizons in which he floated, "I guess you folks would say sayonara at a time like this." He turned away, then turned back again. "If ol' slick decides to drop back to earth from the Great Void, maybe you could let me know."

"Yes, of course," Cassandra answered. "Of course I will. And good luck, Mr. Montana. I sincerely mean that," she said with a catch in her voice, which made Alex sense that she actually might care.

He walked back out through the large mirrored room, his reflection the only other person there, and, as if it really were someone else, he couldn't help taking stock of what he saw. It was how others would remember him, after he was knocked off, he supposed.

Tall and lean, weathered and mean. No, that was wrong. He didn't appear mean exactly; it was more that he had that kind of world-weary expression that passed for sardonic. Women, he had been told often enough, loved that look. He had always found it worked: a squint of one eye, tilt of the head, that sort of thing. No emotion, just the hint of something lying beneath the surface, which they were—if he was lucky—supposed to drag out of him through various forms of affection, preferably physical. The "look" was further abetted by having gray eyes with little gold flecks in them; the little gold flecks were always good for eliciting a bit of conversation and a peek down a bodice as the curious drew in for a closer look. His hair was brown, although being out in the sun a lot had streaked it with equal amounts of blond. He needed a haircut, he supposed, but the little extra length wasn't bad, either. He wondered if they'd give him a haircut before they buried him. Maybe he should save himself the time and the few bucks.

Alex sighed. This whole situation about his impending departure from the planet was making him crazy. The worst part of it was that he was taking it so well, like a layoff from a factory. This wasn't the same, only he couldn't quite get that straight. He was going to be laid out for good, for eternity, unless people came back again as the Buddhists claimed. One thing: if he did come back, Ogata Kenzo was going to be one sorry son of a bitch.

Alex was at the curb, just about to step down, and looking both ways to see if some mad killer behind the wheel was out there ready to pay his last respects, when Cassandra Burke came rushing to his side.

She seemed so much smaller than he had originally thought, he observed, looking down into her face. The blue eyes again enveloped him, and he fought for his most devastating squint, but didn't have the energy to go through with the whole charade. Anyway, he had already made his move, and she didn't want to have a drink with him.

"You forgot to tell me how to get hold of you," she said. "I mean, I assume since they tried to kill you, you're not going back to your old place."

"I'm staying out in the desert," he said. "Out by Palm Springs. There's no address and no phone, just a mountain with a rock that looks like a bird at the top. Off the main road there's a metal road sign without the sign on it. Down that road—it's more of a path—you come to my estate. It's a shack of sorts, with a barn for a garage. That's where I hang out."

"How would I find you then?"

Alex looked off into the distance. "Well, you'd take the main drag to the Springs, look for the mountain with a rock that looks like a bird on top, look for a pole without a sign and just hope for the best, I guess."

"Oh, great," Cassandra said. "You couldn't be just a tad more specific, could you? I mean, it *is* your life we're trying to save here."

Alex thought about it. Nodding, he said, "The stone that looks like a bird? It looks a whole lot like a vulture to me."

He tipped two fingers to his forehead, smiled and sauntered off through the break in the traffic flow. At the other side, he happened to notice Cassandra Burke was still staring after him. Too bad she'd refused the drink. She was a damn good-looking female....

Chapter Two

Cassandra had enough problems of her own without thinking of someone else's. Only she couldn't get the cowboy out of her mind. All the way down Pico and across Cloverfield and into her driveway on Twenty-third Street, the idea of Alex Montana getting rubbed out because of that creep Og taking off—well, his dilemma kept getting tangled up with her own issues of impending doom.

The only feeling of relief came when she saw her house. She loved her house, small as it was, mortgaged up to its eaves. Leaky roof and all, it was hers—and the bank's—and it represented the sum total of many years of striving and sacrifice. The house wasn't merely an adorable fixer-upper, as others might see it, but an emblem of man's triumph over adversity—if magnified to maximum global significance.

The saga of the house went thus. First she was a cocktail waitress who lived in dumpy little apartments where nothing worked, and where the landlord demanded first and last month's rent, plus astronomical cleaning and security deposits, which were never, ever, ever returned no matter how spotless you left the place.

As a cocktail waitress, she was pinched, prodded and propositioned, tipped with hotel keys instead of cash, and followed to her car by men who couldn't stand up straight, much less consummate their lustful intentions.

But each day she told herself to hang on, hang in, and not to hang herself. She told herself all the bad times would be worth the goal, shining somewhere in the great beyond, and sometimes with a glimmer so faint that even she could barely make it out. She considered the indignities and injustices to be merely the temporary sacrifices she was making for what she foresaw as a great and noble cause: the attainment of her teaching credential.

She was a college student and, unlike others of her age who had sold out to computer science degrees or spent their money on capping their teeth to become movie queens or rushed into the corporate fray with certificates in public accounting, *she* was going to serve humanity. She was going to be a teacher. In this way, she could encourage, enflame, expand and enrapture young minds so that in turn they would march out of her classroom like so many King Arthurs and John Kennedys, Martin Luther Kings, Gandhis and Joan of Arcs. Yes, she, Cassandra Burke, would stand at the portal waving, knowing that she and her students would be forever spiritually bonded through their noble intentions.

Except it didn't quite turn out that way.

Oh, some of it did. She got through school. She got a job teaching junior high and was thrilled that her assignment was in an inner-city school rather than in Beverly Hills where her role as an educational savior would undoubtedly be considered superfluous. Anyway, the initial thrill didn't last long.

The fact was, her students kept trying to kill her. Or at the very least, to beat her up or humiliate her. It wasn't anything personal; anyone else brave or stupid enough to teach on the same militarized turf got identical treatment. It was entirely democratic.

Besides this, for all the abuse and sheer terror she endured, she got paid peanuts. Many were the nights when she lay awake wishing she had capped her teeth and gone on the quest of film stardom rather than stupidly trying to educate the future leaders of the world—heaven help it.

Besides the occupational disappointment, there was also the situation with men with which to contend.

The media was screaming headlines about the appallingly low ratio of males to females in the area. She, on the other hand, had plenty of suitors. But they were dull, or stupid, or into themselves, or cheap, or smelled, or dressed funny, or were just plain whacked-out in the emotional department. Plus, she had her standards, and there was no chance of compromise in the matter of her heart. She wasn't settling for any frog. If he was a prince, let him come forth in full regalia. *Then* they'd talk.

So, all in all, it had been a pretty bleak existence for quite some time. Until the house.

The idea of getting her own house came to her when the real estate market was down and foreclosures were happening right and left. Houses that were a quarter of a million dollars were being picked up for half that amount. Houses that were half that amount were going for half of that amount, and so on.

It came to pass that she purchased one of the houses at a fraction of a fraction of its cost. To arrange this, she cashed in her retirement account, took out her personal savings, arranged for a second mortgage, then a third mortgage with an enormous payment—gaily referred to by the lender as a balloon payment, which she later learned meant that whatever you had could disappear into thin air.

The house was her castle; her safe place in the world. It was her husband, her child, her security, her reward for driving the freeway and for suffering the daily abuses of teenage Attila the Huns.

One day, however, after having been mugged outside the grocery store and held captive in her classroom for two hours by a boy who didn't like to be asked questions to which he didn't know the answers, it occurred to her that if she didn't do something fast, she wasn't going to have the opportunity to do anything later.

The next day she went to enroll in a self-defense class, met Og, and a page was turned to a new chapter in her life.

Ogata Kenzo was the most electric personality she had ever run across. He was sometimes so wired up with energy she thought he had been turned by some demon into half man, half neon sign. And at other times a whole different persona emerged. When he began his martial arts classes, there was a deep stillness to him, and behind his eyes Cassandra imagined an ancient soul gazing with omnipotence at the world. No one doubted that Og was a grand master at his craft. Students and Og alike claimed that Ogata Kenzo was on any day, in every way, the equal of Bruce Lee.

Cassandra, herself, came to believe in this, as well as many other of Og's talents—to her current downfall.

The decline began innocently enough. One day she was a student of martial arts. Soon enough she became a gifted student. Eventually she became an unpaid instructor while Og pursued various enterprises unrelated to his martial arts business. They became friends. They almost, but never did, become lovers. That grief, at least, she had been spared by life.

As a friend, Og was elated for her when a rich aunt died and left a smallish but respectable inheritance to be spent however she wished. The sum would cover her balloon payment plus her second mortgage. Cassandra remembered the night well as they toasted to her upcoming financial solvency.

On the following day, however, she instead found herself suddenly a half partner in the Kenzo School of Martial Arts and Protection Agency. She also found herself saying yes to partially funding two fledgling business ventures initiated by Og, who convinced her and several others that their money would be trebled within three months. Now that she had a vested interest in his enterprises, Og next convinced her to quit her teaching job and devote her full energies to running "their" school.

That was six months ago.

And today, as she walked up the flagstone path to her front porch, Ogata Kenzo was gone, and so was her money, and so was her teaching job, and the martial arts school had every chance of being shut down by creditors. And soon, she thought, reality creeping out from behind the waxy-leafed ivy tendrils draping like green storybook mist from the porch's roof, her house would be gone, too.

The cute little balloon payment was due in three weeks.

Inside, she was greeted by her two cats, Hunka and Munka, slinking in through the small cat door in the kitchen. Ralph the canary trilled a manic medley of welcome.

Weary, she fed them all, herself included, and settled into bed early with plenty of time to brood and think of revenges against Og. If he ever did drop back in from the Great Void, as Alex Montana had put it, Og would regret the trip. There was no trick he had under his black belt that would save his fast-traveling little bottom from her. Her wrath was absolutely centered. Her anger was perfectly placed, ready for deployment to effect maximum destruction against one sneaky, low-down, cowardly, cheating human being.

Og, for all his cleverness, had made one big mistake: he had made her his best student.

The last thing she saw before dropping off to sleep, were two beautiful gray eyes with shining sparks of gold, and then a man's face. She turned her face into the pillow and said, "Oh, damn. I don't have enough trouble, already?"

The following day dawned in a gray haze. In Santa Monica almost every day began shrouded by this moist spray of gloom. The city was situated along the Pacific coast. Unfortunately only the rich who owned houses along the shore, and tourists who could afford the hotel rooms where the surf crested majestically—thundering down to the white beaches in a tumultuous crescendo worthy of the love scene in a feature film—were able to experience the area in such romantic terms.

Those who lived inland, like Cassandra, had to deal with the more prosaic aspects of their location, including what was actually nothing more than common fog.

Living in Santa Monica meant contending with the spiritual depression that arose from days beginning as dark forebodings, and the constant vigilance required to scrape off the mold that climbed house frames even while the occupants slept, not to mention the continuing horror of watching the paint on cars being eaten away by the air's salt content.

Still, Santa Monica was home.

Cassandra, more affected by the atmospheric gloom than usual that morning, shoved Hunka and Munka out into the world to ravage the neighbors' garbage cans with their friends, snapped at Ralph the canary for singing when there was nothing to be glad about, and in this mood, took off five minutes too late to be on time to teach her first class.

It didn't matter anyway. There wasn't going to be any class.

Like Druids gathered for a sacrifice, the students stood in a circle on the sidewalk. Their faces bore a mixture of disappointment and expectancy that things would become violent, or at the very least offer some unusually potent dramatic fare. They were grouped around a tall man who, if they had been Druids, would have been the high priest, but who Cassandra recognized at once as a U.S. marshal come to ruin what was left of her life.

He had just finished tacking the notice to the door when she approached. "You're the proprietor?" he asked.

"Only half a proprietor."

"Whatever. You're closed down."

"I kind of got that idea," Cassandra replied. The event was hardly a surprise. In fact, it was long overdue. "Do you mind if I go in there?" she asked. "I mean, I know the law, but I've got some personal things, like a plant and cosmetics, that sort of stuff, and I don't think any creditors are going to be all that interested in my Passion's Promise Flame Red polish, if you know what I mean."

He looked reluctant but relented, following her inside while the Druids gaped with marked disappointment through the glass at them. In her office she gathered the things she had come for while the marshal waited impatiently. She was on her way out when the phone rang. Out of habit she grabbed the call.

For many days to come she wished she hadn't. It was terrifically bad timing.

"Hello," the conversation began quite innocently on her side.

"Li'l gal, sugar, who might this be I'm speaking with?" came the slurred male voice on the other end.

"This is Cassandra Burke. Who is this?" She assumed whoever it was had been drinking heavily.

"Would you be so kind—is this the Kenzo School?"

"Yes, this is the Kenzo School." She nervously eyed the U.S. marshal, who was in turn eyeing her with displeasure. "It was," she corrected as a salute to the officer's authority. He remained unaffected and sullen. Probably, she thought, he had other lives to ruin, and she was mucking up his schedule.

"Well, mighty fine, put him on then. Put on Kenzo. Tell that boy you got Charlie on the horn. Charlie, you hear? He'll know."

Something Cassandra didn't want to know registered at the utterance of the name. Guilt assailed her, and pity, and then annoyance that she had to experience both of the other emotions. Her caller had to be one of the four failures.

"Is that Charlie, as in Big Charlie?" she ventured.

"Sure 'nuf is. Now, missy, I'd appreciate it greatly if you'd call Mr. Kenzo to the—"

"It's really Mr. Ogata. Actually," she said, unable to stop herself, "Kenzo is his first name, but it comes last in Japanese. But no sense in quibbling. I mean, if you like calling him Mr. Kenzo, it wouldn't matter really. Not to me anyway. I just call him Og. Just plain Og." She stopped finally. A leaden misery filled her the way the Santa Monica fog pervaded the neighborhood. "You can call him anything you like because, well, the thing of it is...he's not here. Og's not here, Big Charlie."

Maybe, as she later thought it out, she kept rattling because on some deeper, instinctive level she had a premonition that to hear what Big Charlie was going to say would make an even greater mess of her life.

"Well, that may be, missy, but I've still got to talk to him. I've got an urgent message for Mr. Kenzo. It's a matter of life—"

"And death," Cassandra intoned forlornly.

"—and death that I speak to him," Big Charlie said.

"I'd like to help, but...but I can't." That's what she had said to Alex Montana yesterday. Then it had made her feel as though she were evading some duty in life that had fallen exclusively to her, and now she had the same feeling. It was perplexing and discomforting, and she wished with all her heart that the U.S. marshal would have enough of her dalliance, handcuff her and take her into custody so she wouldn't have to be responsible for anything or anyone—including herself.

"Friedman's bought it. And you've got to let Mr. Kenzo know so he can hustle on out here and save Mr. Montana from the killer or killers."

"What?" Cassandra said, the phone becoming instantly heavier. "What did you say?"

"I said, Jerry Friedman's bought himself stock in that great discount house in the sky. Full-fledged stockholder now, rest his soul."

"Oh, no..." Cassandra sank into her chair. She felt so sorry for Jerry Friedman. Poor, poor henpecked, kindly Jerry with the terrible ogre of a wife. That Doris! "How did it happen?" she asked, her eyes moist.

"Damnedest way to go. Broke his neck, I believe," Big Charlie said expansively, as if relating an exciting fishing story.

"Oh, God. They did that to him? He must have suffered. Oh, poor Jerry." Cassandra formed a complete picture of the murder in her mind, music, Technicolor, poor Jerry lying dead on the pavement, a defeated, crumpled, kindly human being, while three cold-blooded professional killers walked coolly away from the scene. Or maybe it was only one woman. Doris? Alex had said that Jerry was always afraid of Doris doing him in. Cassandra's original picture of the crime was beginning to fuzz, in much the same way as her life had become a cloudy, uncertain blur.

"Well, missy, what the police say is that Jerry fell down a flight of stairs in his apartment."

"Fell?"

"Like I said, that's how the police have it down in their books. Course, I figure it wasn't an accident. Hell, under the circumstances?" Big Charlie's voice lowered. "Gal, I'll give it to you straight. What I reckon is, they're out there, just waiting to pick us off one by one. Then none of us are going to be around to claim any profit or kick up any kind of stink. Of course, Rocky—Alex—is the prime target. He's the golden goose. So they're gonna go get him."

"Who do you think did it?" Cassandra asked, sitting forward in her chair and cradling her head in one hand. "Do you think it might have been Doris?" Somehow the idea of Doris being the killer was far less threatening than the notion of several amorphous professionals lying in wait for Big Charlie and Gordo "the Bomb" Bombolina. And Alex, of course.

"Might have been Doris. For sure, Doris is one mean woman. But, shoot, it could be all of them. The Germans. French. English. Hell's tarnation—anyone who makes cars could be in on it. Personally, I think it's the Ruskies.''

"Big Charlie..." Cassandra said, realizing she had to quickly finish the rest of her sentence. The U.S. marshal was now rapping his large knuckles on the desk. "I'll tell Alex what you said. Don't you worry. I know where to find him, and I'll warn him. You just stay safe yourself."

Big Charlie just managed to thank her before the marshal ushered her out of the room.

Chapter Three

Since it was only February, Cassandra found the desert pleasant to drive through. In fact, had she not been on such a grave mission she might have enjoyed the scenery. To add to her apprehension, she wondered if she would ever even locate her target; or, if she did, would it be after Alex Montana had become the bull's-eye for someone swifter and cleverer than she?

Riddled with all these insecurities, she nevertheless drove on.

The route meandered through mountain passes and down into flat terrain where cacti and palms formed attractive tableaux and splendiferous mobile home parks gave way to housing developments of pink stucco and red tile roofs, surrounded by even more cacti and palms. Then came the signs for the country club manors and the famous spas and the stores on Indian Avenue and hotels fit for kings, and it seemed to Cassandra that she was driving through the pages of a magazine meant for someone else's coffee table. It was depressing.

It was going on two in the afternoon by the time she spotted the stone bird on top of the mountain. Alex Montana was right: it did look like a vulture.

She turned her car down the desert road, a narrow black-topped affair, partly overblown by sand and deeply rutted in spots where the sun had eaten through the tar.

It took maybe ten minutes to get there, but she found what she knew had to be Alex Montana's desert hideout.

If she had expected to be the only visitor, she was wrong. There was a black four-wheel drive wagon with dark-tinted windows parked in front of the house. For a moment she thought her worst fears had come true: the killers had already arrived. But then that seemed too melodramatic, not to mention obvious, what with the black van with opaque windows. Even Hollywood wouldn't stoop to such a blatant foreshadowing of evil. Someone truly dangerous would show up in a yellow dune buggy.

She had just pulled next to the other vehicle when a man came flying out of Alex's front door.

Next came Alex, backward; and soon after, on top of him, another man.

Dumbfounded, she watched as if viewing a movie she had inadvertently walked into. Then the sight of blood on Alex's hand and mouth and a sudden wail of pain sliced through the surrealism and brought her sharply into reality.

Somehow, in what was only an instant, all the months of grueling concentration and physical martial arts practice coalesced in her being, and on automatic, she entered the triangle of three men.

Alex cast her a brief glance of disbelief and horror that she was there, just before he took a terrible blow to the side of his head. At that exact moment, a gun was leveled at him. No thought was necessary; it was totally instinctive. Cassandra took a flying leap and kicked with her foot, dislodging the weapon from the would-be assassin's hands. Spinning around in midair, she kicked again. Then, whirling like a spinning top, she used both hands and legs to fell the two attackers, sending them sprawling. They appeared stunned. She herself could hardly believe it.

As for Alex, he lay moaning on the ground, clutching his shoulder and writhing in what was clearly agonizing pain.

"Oh, my God," Cassandra said, and rushed to him. "Are you all right? You're not dying?"

"Death couldn't be this bad," Alex groaned, looking beyond her. With another groan, he flopped over to reach the gun lying nearby. Twisting in pain, he held it gripped in his fingers, the barrel pointed at the two men who had scrambled back up and stood only an arm's length from Cassandra.

"Now," Alex said, panting through the pain, "you boys run along. You've outworn your welcome here. Know what I mean?" He cocked the gun.

Warily the men backed off, but not without casting looks of malice at Cassandra. A moment later they peeled off in their van in a cloud of dust.

For a time the two of them merely stared at each other, Alex fallen again to one side, Cassandra crouched before him. At last Alex said, "Nice seeing you again."

"Yeah, hi." She didn't know if it was sadistic of her, but squinting in pain that way, she thought he looked extremely attractive. On the other hand, it might have been some motherly instinct surfacing. She wasn't sure. She wasn't sure of anything at the moment, except that he looked good. She tried to think of something else. Like the fact that either of them could have been corpses right now.

"Glad you could—" he took in a breath; the three words were obviously an exertion "—drop by."

"You might have been killed."

"Nah," he said. "No way. By those cream puffs?"

Cassandra saw the look of embarrassment and concerned acknowledgment cross his face. "Right," she agreed, nodding sagely. "Those guys didn't stand a chance against you."

"Hell," he said, shifting his weight slightly and wincing, "I used to take on five or six punks at a time in barroom brawls. Even a couple of steers." He paused reflectively. "Except for maybe that big black one...all of them pieces of cake."

Cassandra nodded. The atmosphere around them grew quiet again. It was an intimate quiet, and thus embarrassing to her, for the more she remained beside him, the more aware of his physical attributes she became. She looked up toward the mountain. The sun was turning white as it drifted behind the top of the stone bird's head. In February the days were shorter; maybe in the desert they ended even more quickly than in Santa Monica. She hadn't been out of Santa Monica fog enough to know.

"I've gotta go to more movies," she said abruptly. "Gotta catch up."

"Movies?"

"I thought bad guys didn't drive black cars anymore. I thought they used pink dune buggies, or yellow, something that goes against type, you know?"

"Nope," Alex said, "black's back in. Backlash against all that wimpy color, I guess."

"I guess," Cassandra conceded without conviction, looking at the stone bird again while her thoughts swirled around in circles.

After a spell of more quiet, Alex said, "I guess I should just say it out plain—thanks. You saved my skin just now."

"No, no..." Cassandra demurred, sensing his discomfort. "I'm sure you could have—"

"Been killed." He stared at her hard, with gray eyes that were at once angry and grateful and humiliated and filled with a sense of bottom-line realism.

"Well," she said, "it was kind of getting to look that way. But, anyway, that's my line of work—the hero business."

Alex nodded. "Nice job. Have you ever considered some healthier line of work, maybe?"

"Like waiting tables or teaching, you mean?"

"Sounds like a plan," he said, and tried to get up but couldn't make it.

"Did them both," Cassandra replied. Offering him her arm and a left shoulder to lean on, she helped raise him. "Waiting tables made me black and blue, and teaching almost made me a vital statistic. Thanks, but I'll take my chances in back alleys and desert brawls." It sounded tough; it sounded cool; she thought it sounded good, all in all. The only problem was, she'd really been frightened silly by what had gone down that afternoon. She really could have been killed! But Alex Montana looked—at least physically—far worse than she did, so offering him a sense of security was a kindness she was tacking on to the basic service for free. Og would have done the same himself—if he were here, which the louse was not, Cassandra reminded herself. Only Og really was tough and cool. Og's big drawback was that he was never around when being tough and cool counted.

Together, she and Alex limped back into his shack. By the time she lowered him onto his bed, she was covered with his blood.

Somehow the blood shocked her. She remembered seeing it in the beginning. Then, for some reason, during the fight, and then afterward, she hadn't really been paying attention, although now, with it all over the place, she couldn't imagine how it could have been overlooked. At first she had been too frightened and preoccupied. Afterward, well, there had been Alex. His face had filled her mind to the exclusion of all else. Now, however, seeing the red stain on her clothes and arm, plus on Alex, she began to waver, and darkness closed down on her. Pitching forward, she was caught and roused by Alex out of what was going to be a full-fledged faint.

"Oh, God...oh, God..." he moaned as she fell into him.

"Oh..." she gasped in turn, seeing the look of agony contort his face. "I'm so sorry..." But she was at an awkward angle, half lying on top of him, a quarter in the air, and another quarter of her frame touching the thin mattress. Her attempt to rise was a fiasco. She toppled even more heavily against him.

"You're killing me, woman!" he shouted.

"I'm sorry, I'm so sorry," Cassandra muttered, and struggled away, this time successfully.

"You work for the other side?" He gave a gasp, and with a monumental effort managed to position himself on his back. He was breathing hard. Turning his head sideways, he softened. "Oh, don't cry," he said. "For pity's sake, woman, at least spare me that."

"I'm not crying," Cassandra said, and sniffed. She wiped away a matching set of tears dribbling down both cheeks.

"Hey," he said, "come here."

"No, I'm fine. I'm perfectly all right." Cassandra looked down at the blood on her skirt and noticed the kick had ripped a big split up the side, from which one leg was entirely exposed. A quick glance showed that Alex Montana was also aware of the expanse of lightly tanned skin.

"Of course, and I'm impressed. I know you're forged of iron," he said with mock defensiveness. "I just want to shake your hand." With effort he extended his arm to her.

Cassandra hesitated, then decided to be a sport and reached for his hand, which clasped hers tightly and in a surprisingly fluid move, pulled inward. She had no alternative but to follow along on the journey.

It ended against Alex's chest, and he kissed her on the mouth. For a moment it felt so good, that kiss, that she forgot they were almost complete strangers. His hand was traveling up the length of her leg. When she realized she was responding to more than the kiss, to his entire body, she stiffened and pushed herself away. It wasn't hard to accomplish. He groaned again and cursed beneath his breath as her elbow stuck him in the ribs.

"Sorry," he said with something approximating a wicked grin. "I just needed to see if all the parts still worked okay."

"They do," Cassandra said sullenly. "Although I doubt you have the steam to keep them in operation long. And just for the record, physical therapy is not in my line of work." There were times, like the present, when looking at him lying there, she wished she didn't have such high standards. Was it really and truly necessary to have a man know your soul before you let him get acquainted with your outer extremities? Anyway, it was a theoretical question. The moment of burgeoning passion between two beat-up human beings had dwindled to conversation.

"Yeah..." he said, and a shadow of a thought darkened his expression. "Your line of work is to keep crippled hot dogs like me alive."

"You're not crippled," she said.

"Might as well be," Alex sighed. "Might sure as hell be..." He looked at her. "The truth is, I'm impressed. You did real good, lady. Seriously," he said again when it appeared she was going to object. "You were really some kind of tigress out there. You ever lose a fight?"

She thought of playing out the charade in her favor; certainly it might keep him in line. In the end, she gave into her honest streak, which she had come to consider a character defect. Like the Grand Canyon, integrity cut a deep swath down the length of her personality. Into this cavernous expanse she often fell, became hopelessly lost, and many times, barely survived the expedition.

"I've never had a fight," Cassandra said with a self-deprecating smirk.

"You're serious? You *are* serious." Alex looked as if he didn't want her to be.

"I'd say 'dead serious,' only it might not be appropriate," Cassandra said. "But, yes, that little item of confidentiality is the God's honest truth. You can even have my Scout's pledge on it."

Alex closed his eyes. "Then I really could have met my maker."

"Sure could have," Cassandra agreed cheerily. No one could have been more surprised by her valiant performance than she. It was the first time outside the classroom she had ever put into practice the methods she had been trained to use. Now, in retrospect, she supposed she had perceived the lessons more as a psychological talisman against being attacked than as preparation for actual physical combat.

"Anyway, I'm glad you dropped by. Means that you've got some good news for me. The man's shown himself."

For the first time since her arrival, she remembered her assignment. Under present circumstances, half the news she bore was even more poignant, and the other half more frightening, than it had been before she'd set off. Now she understood the benefit of telegrams.

It would have read: *Mr. Alex Montana. Your good friend, poor Jerry Friedman, is dead. Some killers got him. Now you are being hunted. Hide. Run for your life. Best regards.*

Alex was watching her. Scowling, he said, "Okay, so you've got something to tell me and it isn't good. Your partner says he doesn't want to take on the rough stuff, huh?"

"Uh, no..." she said. "That's not exactly it. It's, uh, something else." How was she going to tell him? Before, Alex was more of a client. She had felt morally and ethically responsible for helping him. But now...now...well, he had bled on her for crying out loud. And she had looked into his eyes. And it was somehow all very wonderful and frightening and confusing. She didn't really mind losing her life so much as she now hated the idea of hurting him with what she had to say.

"Are you going to tell me what's going on?"

Her eyes drifted around the place. "Well, I got a call this morning." She didn't really want to tell him at all. It was like kicking someone who was already down. What furniture there was, was also down. The shack must have been a prospector's place at one time. It was small and dark and slightly damp, in spite of being in the desert. There was an old wood-burning stove in one corner, and the single double bed where Alex lay was against another wall. In the center of the room there was a table tipped on its side and three overturned chairs. On the floor were some eating utensils and tin plates and scraps of food.

"You don't have anything to drink around here, do you?" she asked. "For medicinal purposes, of course."

"Over there." He jerked his head in the direction of a crude cupboard affixed to the wall.

Cassandra felt him watching her as she crossed the room, pulled a bottle of whiskey out, then rummaged around until she found a clean glass and a tin mug in the same cabinet. Filling them, she brought them both back, gave Alex Montana one and sat beside him on the edge of the bed.

"To life," she said, and they clinked glass and tin together.

Cassandra took a deep swallow and thought she would die from it. When the burning stopped, she said, "I'm afraid it's bad news, Mr. Montana."

"Why did I kind of figure that?"

"How about another drink?" she suggested.

"Take a deep breath and just say it."

"Okay. Okay." She took a breath. "This morning I got a call from your investor friend, Big Charlie. He said that Jerry Friedman has died. Was killed, or something."

Alex stared at her. "Or something?"

"Well, he's not alive anymore," she said. It sounded so crazy, as if she were discussing a tire that had gone flat— or a pickle jar that had busted. She was talking about the end of a man's life, and all it boiled down to was this one lousy sentence. No trumpets. No screams and crying. Just having a few letters strung together by a woman who didn't even know the guy didn't seem right. But there it was.

She went on because there wasn't anything else to do. "And Big Charlie wasn't certain about it being an accident or a deliberate act of murder. That is, Jerry fell down the stairs and broke his neck. Big Charlie wanted you to know because he was afraid they'd be coming after you next. I guess he was right." She paused. "I'm so sorry, Alex."

For the longest while Alex didn't say anything. He took a couple of swallows of whiskey, then one long swig, which finished the mug off.

Cassandra poured him another shot, and he drank that one down as well. Then he lay back with his head on the pillow, remaining silent. It was as if Cassandra could hear voices—small, dim voices from another space and another time—come from whatever memories Alex must have been experiencing. Jerry Friedman and Alex talking. Jerry Friedman and Alex laughing. The other two, Gordo and Big Charlie, joining up with Jerry and Alex. All the dreams, the plans. Cassandra shut her eyes tightly, trying to keep out Alex's sorrow. She had enough of her own.

"Okay," Alex said. "Okay, thanks. For telling me." His voice was very tight, and there was an infinity of grief behind the control.

Cassandra reached forward for his glass, but he stopped her with a look. She poured herself another quarter glass. The bottle was running out. So was her fortitude.

By now it was almost dark in the cabin, and Cassandra had trouble making out the expression on Alex's face. But the eyes were easy enough to see. They gleamed brightly even in the dusky interior. From the open door a stream of fading daylight fell upon the slanted plank floor. The light seemed to travel like an arrow to the bed, illuminating Alex's form in a soft, glowing haze. He was crying, she realized with tenderness. At that moment Alex turned his head away. She saw his shoulders heave slightly, then his body tense as he gathered control of his feelings.

"I'm so, so sorry," she said, and truly meant it. "I didn't know him, but crazy as it may seem, I felt like I did. It was like he was my friend, too."

"Two weeks," Alex said. "If it's the last thing I do, I'm going to stay alive for two weeks. Me and that engine are going to be in the Los Angeles Sports Arena. I owe Jerry. He believed in me. I'm sure as hell not going to let him down. Wherever he is now."

What she had told Alex was true. She had never even known of the man until the day before, but she felt as if someone she had loved for many years had been severely wronged, not to mention shortchanged. Reaching out, she touched Alex's arm lightly, "You'll do it," she said through her own tears. "I just know you will."

And then the thing happened that she never, not ever, in a thousand years would have believed possible. This man, lying flat on his back, who was not in any way imaginable a prince, but instead a tattered, bloodied specimen of a frog with nothing but a dream to recommend him, was holding her in his arms and kissing her.

And she was kissing back.

It was not the most vigorous love scene in the history of erotica, but it might have been the most tender. They were both kissing and crying and holding each other. And she was loving all of it.

He lay flat, with her on top of him, and his hands traveled like an electric current along her body, seeming to desire her as much for her physical warmth as for the emotion she felt spilling out of her, wave upon wave, of love and joy and protectiveness. And, then, of course... desire.

There was a sculpted perfection to his body. It was as hard and perfect in proportion as the Grecian statues she had seen in museums. And natural. There was, most of all, the comfortable, assured naturalness of him that made her respond so fully to the intimacies she would have refused any other man. Even her prince, perhaps. But she didn't think of him now. She couldn't think at all; she could only feel.

They spoke little, but now and again he would sigh, and kissing her, would say her name as if each time were the first. "Cassandra...Cassandra..." In the quiet of the small room, his voice might have been the soft flow of desert breeze through the wooden slats of the cottage.

His hands played softly over her blouse, teasing, then releasing each button one by one as he kissed her neck and the circular hollow at its base. Her breath came more ragged now. Whatever breathing skills she had been taught in her classes on centering the flow of her breath for protection were lost entirely to the melting sensation of the rest of her body.

Her bra appeared no more than a pink lace feather against her swelling breasts as Alex slipped the blouse off her shoulders. Over the lace she felt the searing warmth of his hands, and then slowly, lowering each strap separately, he discarded the restraining fabric. His tongue was a hot lick against her flesh, maddening her. She moved into him, encouraging him to take her more fully, which he did. Her fingers found him, and he trembled at her touch, no longer the one in control.

Urgently he unfastened her skirt at the waist and insistently worked it down, with slight help from her, over her buttocks and past her thighs until she wriggled free from the cloth. His hands found the lacy triangle of her panties and pulled them away, confident fingers exploring and dissolving whatever remaining reservations she still harbored. No more did it matter to her what happened; only that she make love fully and completely with this man. Time and place had no more meaning. Princes and frogs were inconsequential. There was only him. And her. And now.

The fire in her was almost frightening. She had not known. Even she had not known! Beneath the cool facade that had allowed her to fend off the hands of drunken customers and to defeat men twice her size in the martial arts studio was a woman whose passion bore the force of whirlpools and riptides. The hunger she had kept hidden, even from herself, streaked through her body and soul, sizzling like an exploding supernova as Alex moved his mouth against her flesh.

Now and then flickers of confusion and a sense of fear that she had lost her mind, her standards, her body, and most likely her soul, to this man whose touch was driving her to the brink of some unknown place, would invade the ecstasy.

But it was too late by far to stop.

She moved up, allowing him to enter, and the silken smoothness of their joining caused them both to shiver, a gasp rising in her at the same time as a low moan issued from him. The heat grew, the urgent demand they felt for each other building, and finally the moment arose when there were no longer two bodies moving in tandem, just one joyous experience of melding into each other.

There was the raw force of their physical desire for each other, but there was something else, too. The sweetness. It was almost unbearably intimate, the experience they had shared, and she knew that he felt the frightening intensity of that softness just as she did. It made what they had together real; it wasn't just flesh joining in a desert cabin— it was *them*, touching each other on a thousand different levels. The intensity of their bonding was surprising and shattering. Something in that dark quiet room had occurred that neither of them had foreseen as possible.

Afterward they lay side by side, Cassandra partially clothed, Alex still wearing his bloodied shirt, undone. His pants had been cast aside, and now a sheet covered his torso. It was almost dark in the room.

Cassandra listened to his breathing. It wasn't regular, and she realized the exertion must have taken its toll on him. With that tender protectiveness sweeping over her, she wanted to touch him again. But she didn't. It was too confusing. The sex hadn't been just sex; it had been something more. God, she thought, it had rocked her to her very core! But how was that possible? Emotions like that came when you knew a person well, when you shared good times and bad times, when you had some history together, for God's sake!

He reached for her hand suddenly, as if afraid she had left. In a way she had. She was pulling out of the dream they had so recently shared.

"Don't . . ." she said, and he moved his hand away. She was sorry, but that was the way it had to be. Because none of this was making any sense. It wasn't real. *But it was real!* "I'd better get going." She started to rise.

This time he drew her back with a forceful tug.

"Stay," he said.

"I can't." She didn't trust herself to look at him. She'd be lost. He had that kind of effect on her.

"Why?"

"I've got cats."

"Cats can take care of themselves."

"There's Ralph."

"Ralph?" His voice had become tight.

She smiled in spite of herself, knowing what he was thinking. "Ralph the canary. He's locked up. He can't do much for himself."

"I know the feeling."

Alex was staring at her. She couldn't see him clearly in the dark, but she felt his eyes as certainly as she had felt him enter her body before. He was making her feel guilty.

"Look," she said, desperation tightening around her like a noose, "I came here to give you a message. Along the way, I got into a fight, and thank God, won it. Unexpectedly we had sex—"

"Sex?" He laughed, but it wasn't out of humor.

They both entered a mutual silence.

"We made love. Okay, better?" she said, but not without sarcasm.

And of course he didn't answer. The silence was condemning. What did he want from her? Did he think she would believe they had fallen madly in love? She may have been a pretty dumb bunny in her days, but even for her there was a limit to stupidity.

She went on. "Beyond what I have already done, I don't know what to do for you, or with you." She stood up, feeling frantic to get out of his presence. She needed some sort of stability in her life, and being around him was making the world slant at odd angles. "Is there some sort of a light in this place, or do you rub sticks together when you want to see things?"

"For openers, I need to go to a hospital," Alex said in a flat tone. "There are matches in that drawer. And a lantern over there."

Cassandra obeyed. While he fiddled with the lantern, she stood over him. Soon a glow filled the room. She looked down and said, "Really, you need to go to a hospital?"

He gave her a look of disbelief. "Yes. Really. If I weren't such a super kind of guy, I might be squealing around this shack, complaining like the devil. But that's just the kind of stuff I'm made out of, okay? Only even I have a limit."

"You seemed all right when we—"

"Yeah, well, ever read those stories about people who can suddenly lift cars when they have to?"

"It was like that, huh?"

"Yeah, like that." There was no warmth in his expression. She had hurt him. She had really wounded him in a way that went far beyond what his assailants had accomplished earlier.

She didn't know if she was glad about that revelation or not. She understood now what that feeling between them had been, even if he was thinking it was something else. No, it wasn't impersonal lust, but it wasn't necessarily falling in love forever after, either. What it had been was dire loneliness and the sense of human mortality bearing down on them. Old Jerry Friedman was up there teaching them a lesson or two about what was important in life, and what wasn't worth the time and trouble. "Take what you got, when you got it, folks. And run with it. While you can, while you can..."

"Okay," she said. "I'll drive you into Palm Springs. They've got to have some ritzy class-A hospital that'll do for the likes of your rough-tough stuff, Mr. Montana."

They repaired themselves for entry into the real world again and set off for her car.

The moon was out, and the landscape was a pale wash of blue and silver. A dry desert wind had risen and was now blowing out of the canyons. Groups of tumbleweed rustled by like people traveling past into the night.

Cassandra had her car door open when she noted that Alex was hanging back. He had stopped completely, in fact, and was staring at the vehicle. "No, way," he said.

"No way, what?"

"That thing'll finish me off. I get into it, it's the end."

"Ah," she said, understanding. It was a sports car, an old lime-green Fiat Spider, which didn't run in the rain. Even under normal circumstances, a man Alex Montana's size would be hard-pressed to pretzel himself into it. He was right—the Fiat could kill him.

Instead, Cassandra found herself behind the wheel of an old jalopy, powered by none other than the wonder engine that was soon to revolutionize the world.

As they drove in silence down the desert road, Cassandra had the sinking feeling that the man beside her had also come to revolutionize her life. She didn't know if that was a good thing, or if it was going to mean serious trouble. She glanced sideways at Alex and found him watching her.

He smiled. "Hi," he said.

She couldn't help but smile back.

Chapter Four

The hospital rose against the purple desert night like a swank nightclub. Lit from below in yellow and pink light, palm trees stood like gargantuan lollipops along the circular drive. The building's front was itself a broad concave sweep of glass. It was brightly lighted from within, and Cassandra thought it resembled the overbright smile of a politician.

She pulled the car up to the front entrance where a long gold Mercedes had just parked. A woman in a white fur coat left the passenger side of the Mercedes and trotted to the door with a load of white roses in clear cellophane.

"Okay," Cassandra said. "You're here. Still in one piece," she added pointedly.

"God Almighty..." Alex moaned with a forebearing tone of martyrdom. Beneath his breath he added what sounded like a fervent curse, but Cassandra couldn't make out the details. Anyway, he made her mad.

"What now? What complaint do you have *now*? We aren't even moving!" she snapped. She gripped the steering wheel with two hands, wishing she had him by the neck instead. But she didn't dare to look his way. She might cry. She was tired and frustrated, caught between anger at his remarks and pity for both their positions. Anger had the immediate edge, however—another disparaging remark from him and she would deprive the would-be killers of their livelihood and finish him off herself.

"Nothing," he said. "Forget it."

"No, no," Cassandra pressed, now looking at him with malice. "You said 'God Almighty,' and you muttered under your breath. That means something. I want to know what."

"You want to know what?" He shifted around slightly but fell back against the seat just as fast, his face registering pain. He took a moment, then turning only his head, said, "I'll tell you what, okay?"

"Yeah, okay. Tell me."

"You drive like a maniac."

"A maniac! I drive like a maniac?"

"Not only do you drive like some kind of speed-crazed, lead-footed psycho, but you stop like one. If I didn't already have problems enough, you've added whiplash to my misery."

"Oh? Oh, really?" Cassandra didn't know if she was more hurt or furious. Alex had done nothing but complain about her driving the entire way, and as driving was one thing she particularly prided herself on, she hadn't liked his comments one little bit.

"Absolutely," Alex confirmed, staring her down with equal intensity.

"Well, I've got a word or two for you, too, cowboy."

"Fine, fine . . . give 'em both to me."

"It so happens I had a few problems of my own before you came sashaying into my life with your fancy boots and big demands. It's not like you've done me any big favors. Ever since you've hit the scene, I've almost been killed, I've ruined my skirt, I'm out here in the middle of the night in the desert, blood on my blouse, my hair filled with sand, nothing to eat since this morning, my cats probably hate me, and God only knows what Ralph must be feeling. It may also interest you to know that until you we led what society might consider a normal life-style. In a way," she added, being fair.

To be accurate, since she had hooked up with Og, things had more or less disintegrated in the normal department. But until her fateful meeting with Og, they—the cats and Ralph and she—*had* led a nice peaceful life: dinner on time, twice-monthly routine for paying bills, grocery shopping on Saturday, laundry on Tuesday, plants watered on a regular basis, the same faces entertained on a prescheduled rotational basis. It had all been so nice and ordinary—and most of all—safe. All she had lacked was her prince.

She and Alex stared at each other for a long, silent, hostile moment.

"Fact," Alex said finally, obviously having formulated some new platform from which to launch a further assault, "you're half owner of that sad excuse for a protection agency. Which means you owe me." He pointed an accusatory index finger her way. "We're talking legal now. I paid, you deliver."

"Og owes you!" she protested, affronted at having her integrity challenged.

"Half of Og owes me. The other half is you, sweetheart, and I've got a right to collect on my dollar." He was breathing a little unevenly.

"Are you okay?" Cassandra asked, forgetting their differences for a moment.

"You care?" He raised his eyebrows disbelievingly.

"I just don't want you dying on me, okay? I mean, frankly, my day has been bad enough already. I don't think I can deal with a corpse in the front seat."

"No problem. You just drive this heap to a car wash and tell them to vacuum me out of your life."

"Would but they could."

"I'm in pain, got it?"

"You *are* a pain. You are definitely not funny."

"It so happens I feel like a branding iron is being poked in my shoulder. Insulting you and cracking macabre jokes just lightens the load a little."

"Come on," Cassandra said, "let's go in." She nodded to the front of the hospital. "I don't have the money for a car wash."

"First, we're going to settle this."

She reached for the door handle. "We'll settle it later."

"I may be dead later," Alex said firmly without humor. More softly he said, "We'll settle it now. There's not much I can do in life anymore, and if I have this opportunity to win a verbal battle with a pigheaded, shortsighted, mean-tempered female, I'm taking it." The speech, which had been fairly animated, took its toll. He shuddered slightly from the exertion of energy, then went on.

"You wanted things nice and safe, just to collect money on your investment in that sorry excuse for a protection agency, but I think you overlooked something. Protection means, by its very nature, that some kind of danger's involved. A coin's got two sides, baby. You make a toss, you don't just get heads. Sometimes it happens that tails comes up on a flip, and that's what you're left with. Now you can run out of the deal, just like your pal Kenzo. That's up to you. God knows I'm not in any position to chase you down. But I paid for service. That means I paid for this ride. I did my part as a client, see. Now you get to decide here and now what you're going to do. You're either in the game, or you're out.''

"Precisely the point. It's not a game,'' Cassandra objected. ''This is dangerous. You're right about that, anyway.''

"That doesn't answer my question.''

"Am I in or out? I'd like to be gone from the whole situation—not in, not out, just gone.''

"Well, you don't exactly have that option. You're here.''

"Has it ever occurred to you that I'm not really equipped to handle this kind of a deal?''

"Baby, you could have fooled me today.''

"And do you ever have it wrong. You want to know something? I was frightened. Frightened to death when it was over. And I still am. I did what I did at the time, but I didn't think about it. Now that I'm thinking about it— even the likelihood of that kind of scene happening again—my blood turns to solid ice and my brain locks up.''

"All you've just told me is you're human.''

"I'm Jell-O! Jell-O is not human. Jell-O is Jell-O! It wobbles if you blow on it hard. It melts if it gets too near the heat.''

"So,'' Alex said, ''you're out? In a word—yes, no or what?''

What? At that moment Cassandra felt as if all nature were being held in suspension while she formulated her response. This was not a question; this was a test of cosmic significance. Worlds might perish. Civilizations would crumble. If she said she wanted no part in Alex Montana's miserable situation, maybe her soul would burn in

hell for all eternity; or, on a happier note, maybe there was
no hell. Maybe she could say no and merely live a long and
happy and selfish life. Even her financial struggles didn't
seem quite so monumental now in light of this other situation—the likelihood of becoming a corpse.

It was better, she felt, to take a sure thing. She wasn't
certain about souls or hell. But she knew she had a body,
and she knew if she were to take on the job of protecting
this grump of a cowboy, she'd probably lose that body of
hers to a bullet.

One word: yes, or no. Very simple. That's all that was
needed. She could say yes and be in hot water, and maybe
in the near future be fitted for a nice padded coffin. Or,
one other little word, no, and she could be set free of all
responsibility and live a long, full life with Hunka and
Munka and Ralph, waiting for her prince to come.

"No," she said, choosing the cats, Ralph and her elu-
sive lover.

The word hung there between them. It seemed to grow,
no, No, NO, *NO-O-O-O*. And then like a balloon it
popped. The air became suddenly cold.

"Then no it is!" Alex said energetically, and reached for
the door handle.

Just like that. She was off the hook. There was a buoy-
ant feeling of relief as she opened her own door. But there
was a terrible sadness, too. Oddly it was she who felt
abandoned. The feeling was heavier than Alex as she sup-
ported him up the shallow steps leading to the hospital.

The receptionist at the information desk was deeply
tanned. She might have been a concierge in a ritzy hotel.
Her nails were long and manicured and, Cassandra knew,
fake. The woman wore a lovely hot pink knit suit. There
was a lavish arrangement of fresh flowers on the side of the
desk. The flowers, like the woman, appeared artificial.

Large tropical trees grew in rich pockets of dark earth, interrupting the flow of the thick blue carpeting underfoot. It was hard to tell if the trees were real; even the dirt might have been imitation. It was so black, like granules of velvet. Everything in the place looked too good, as if life had been juiced up to be something more than it actually was.

Cassandra stood patiently alongside while Alex filled out an information form that would allow him to be admitted to the emergency room. There his shoulder would be snapped back into place. Maybe then he would stop his complaining.

All of this would soon be over. She would go home and take a long bath. She would look for a job in the morning. Eventually she would find something satisfactory. A nice, routine, safe existence would flow from one day to the next. And then, on one of those days when she least expected, Prince Perfect would come galloping into her line of vision, sweep her up into his arms and off they would go into the sunset. That was the way things truly happened. Good things came about right on schedule when they were destined, not too soon, not too late. Regardless of the myths to the contrary, propagated by the deluded advocates of assertiveness training seminars, Cassandra felt she could relax and wait rather than go out with a butterfly net and catch Mr. Right.

"There you go," Alex said, handing the completed card to the receptionist. "Just so we have a king-size bed and a view of the pool."

"What?" the woman asked.

"Nothing," Cassandra said quickly. "It's the pain. It makes him say stupid things."

"Oh," the woman commented.

Alex smiled broadly. Cassandra grabbed him by the elbow. They headed down the hallway, more of a grand concourse actually, to the emergency room. "That was really unnecessary," Cassandra said.

"You mean my cleverly veiled proposition about the bed?"

"Yes."

"She was a dim bulb. She didn't get it anyway."

"Well, I did. And it was humiliating to me."

"Oh," he said. "Sorry, then. I just didn't realize. Hating each other obviously means we can't sleep together again."

Cassandra stopped. Alex hung back, too, the light of pure innocence shining forth from his eyes. Or maybe it was pain. She was too tired and confused to deal with his psychological and physical defects anymore. "After you get patched up and I drive you home, you are never, never, going to see me again."

"You're certain about that?"

"Currently I am sure of very little, but of this one thing I'm absolutely certain. I no longer work at the studio, and I've an unlisted number. You couldn't even find me."

"If I wanted to..."

"If you wanted to..."

"I don't want to," he said. "However," he went on, "if I got to thinking about this afternoon, I could have a change of heart."

Cassandra sent him a look of disgust. "Then that's all you could do, just think about it." She started forward again. "There it is," she said, nodding to the sign identifying the emergency room.

"Am I to take it that this afternoon was not a major moment in her life?" Alex mused aloud.

"Look," she said, speaking under her breath as a couple of orderlies passed them, "I think it's kind of sophomoric to give out gold stars for performance."

"Ah!" he said delightedly. "I warrant a gold star!"

"It was what it was. It happened. Now it's over. Can we forget this topic? Please?"

"I'd like to clarify something first."

She rolled her eyes. "What might that be?"

"It wasn't a performance—at least not on my part."

"Fine. Now you've told me. So can we talk about something pleasant? Like broken bones, or killers, or something?"

"No," he said. They had almost reached the door to the emergency room. "I don't want to forget this afternoon. Notice how nice I'm being? I'm speaking in euphemisms. I'm showing regard for your delicate sensibilities. I could have merely said, 'Great sex.'"

"Will you give me a break!" She walked faster toward the sign, feeling that it *was* an emergency.

"Will you give me the truth?" Alex demanded, and swung her around by the shoulder.

At that moment a blue light flashed above the door and a low piercing wail filled the corridor. From a side aisle doctors, nurses and a crew of orderlies rushed by, along with two aluminum gurneys transporting what appeared to be traffic casualties.

Cassandra and Alex stepped back as the parade of medics flew through the double doors.

From within they heard muted voices, but in the corridor there was again that cushioned quiet that denied the reality of the building's actual purpose. It was not a hotel, not a nightclub; the magnificent edifice was a battlefield where life and death jousted.

In the aftermath of the drama, they could only look at each other, their differences somehow viewed from an altered perspective. Shame, along with a strange sense of heroic joy, assailed Cassandra. There was something about seeing a person lying there, fighting for life, that showed Life for what it truly was: a magnificent, precious ongoing miracle. Life was so taken for granted. She took it for granted. It was discounted. She discounted it. It was squandered and belittled because it seemed always to be there. *Seemed.* But it was not so. Life did not last forever. And when a person realized that, then perhaps that was when one truly began to live. There was something in that realization that went beyond the intellectual. It touched the emotions. It humbled her.

Her heart sent a prayer to the unknown beings who had just been wheeled past, helpless but for their will to live. She wanted them to survive.

She thought about the question he had posed just before the interruption. What if she told him how she really felt about that afternoon?

"I'm going in," Alex said. "Maybe in the middle of all the blood and guts they can find the time to patch up an old cowhand."

What if he knew she had never known anything could exist in the world, especially for her, that was close to what they had shared today? But all she said was, "You ought to be a welcome relief."

"At least I'll be welcome somewhere."

What if he knew she was terribly confused by her passionate response to him, a man who was nothing more than a stranger, that she wished to drop the whole matter before her life became even more muddled? What if?

"Do you want me to come in with you?" she asked.

"No, I'd like to keep what dignity I've got intact. It's not a pretty picture, seeing a man having his bones rearranged. They'll tape me up, I guess. So I can make it back to the lobby on my own steam, if you want to hang out there."

"Sure," she said, relieved to have some emotional breathing space. "I'll just wait, then." Alex turned and was pushing through to the other side of the emergency room when she called, "Alex!"

He paused, turning his head. "Yeah?"

Cassandra was looking at him hard, trying to see if there was anything princely about him before declaring herself. There was nothing, not a damn clue, to make her believe there could be any more to a relationship with Alex "Rocky" Montana than the trouble he had already caused her and the physical bliss of their time in bed. "I hope it doesn't hurt too much," she said.

He looked at her strangely, as if waiting for more to come. When it didn't, he nodded, and with a smile said, "Baby, some things hurt more than others . . . and sometimes physical stuff ain't necessarily the worst of what comes down the pike. If you know what I mean . . ." Then he was gone.

Cassandra stared at the spot he had so recently inhabited. She figured she knew exactly what he meant. She really did feel miserable. She couldn't say exactly why, or maybe she didn't want to admit the reason, but she knew the feeling had nothing to do with open wounds of the physical variety. Life was so confusing. . . .

Chapter Five

The ride back to Alex's shack began like a piece of heaven. For one thing, Cassandra found she had been right: Alex's disposition had been greatly improved by the doctors' ministrations.

They had—as he had projected—sprung his bones back into proper order. He had been securely taped up as well to keep anything from popping back out again, she supposed. Now he sat rather stiffly beside her, bound as he was around his midriff and bad shoulder, but his face had relaxed into the original, more pleasing expression he had worn when they'd initially met.

Was their first encounter only yesterday? It seemed like a year.

She was driving again, only this time Alex sat as quiet as a lamb, looking out at the dark countryside. Now and then he would yawn or scratch his ear. If not for that, she might have thought him asleep. Or dead, she thought blackly, reminding herself that he was not an ordinary passenger and this was not the usual kind of drive. But for now only the strange hum of the motor insinuated itself into their silent company.

Stealing a quick glance his way, Cassandra had to give Alex Montana his due. He was a handsome man. There was something imperfectly perfect about him. Strong jaw, nose straight, not too long, nor short, a face generally reminiscent of some noble Roman patriot whose likeness was chiseled into now-disintegrated marble. If Alex had been so much as a smidgeon better looking, it would have taken away the aura of strength. And, conversely, if he had come across any more rugged, it would have destroyed the undercurrent of vulnerability he conveyed. Physically, she had to admit, he was damn near a perfect male specimen—if a woman was given to fits of weakness over twinkles of starlight behind thick lashes, a faintly crooked smile outlining a row of teeth any movie star would have killed for and an easy, self-assured way of moving the body.

That body. A wave of prickles traversed her spine as she recalled the afternoon's erotic idyll. Superficial stuff to be summarily dismissed, she cautioned herself, nothing to warrant a major emotional commitment. Take away the looks, the magnetic attraction of two bodies consisting of mostly water molecules, and what was left to hang a full-blown relationship on?

That was entirely the problem: the "what was left." It was that softness behind the outer shell of Alex Montana that was most alluring. In fact, if he hadn't been such an easy man to find aggravating, she would have been in seriously dangerous emotional territory.

But, as it was, he constantly said things that put her off, did things that did not mesh with her vision of how life was to be lived forever after in her ivy-covered cottage and created an environment of such general uneasiness that she couldn't even begin to consider him as a legitimate suitor. Granted, he had those few good things going for him; still, he wasn't her type. She had known her type since she was twelve, and he wasn't it. Definitely not.

It was a shame he had to cause himself and everyone else so much trouble. Life would be so much easier for him if he developed a few social skills of the polished variety. He was undoubtedly one of those males who didn't know how to connect with a woman and was thus destined to remain lonely, misunderstood and bewildered throughout his life. She knew the scenario well from observation of other case histories related by her female friends. At the very best Alex Montana was likely to marry some poor woman who would be his inferior, just to have someone in his bed and to make him feel in step with the rest of the world's population. Eventually, wounded by his disinterest, the unfortunate woman would send him on his way. Of course, after that, he would be so embittered he'd just give up trying to connect with anyone—unless it was in a motel for an hour or two.

For all she knew he might already have an ex-wife and three kids holed up in some ranch house in Montana or Oregon. But as soon as she thought it, the idea didn't sit well. There was something untamed and individualistic about Alex Montana; that was her impression anyway. The notion of him having such a prosaic history was a disappointment to her. Wasn't it enough that she'd had to swallow the truth about Santa Claus and the Easter Bunny? To have Alex's image crushed, too, seemed cruel. Rather, she preferred to think of him as some reckless rotter, chasing women and booze and steers over the planet. There weren't too many of his kind left in the world. As an endangered species, he ought to be preserved for posterity.

This last thought triggered the unwelcome voice of responsibility in her. She didn't want to be involved with wild men like Alex and Og.

She had her own troubles. Sad as Alex's case might be, she wasn't a social worker or a shrink. He'd just have to fend for himself, take his own lumps from life, like the rest of the world. Didn't she have problems enough of her own without worrying about someone else—and a man she barely knew to boot? It annoyed her, this course of thought. Any way you cut it, Alex Montana was occupying far too much of her time.

Well, soon she'd be rid of him—maybe in another half hour—and by next week she'd be thinking back upon her encounters with Alex Montana as nothing more than incidents in a strange dream.

They had driven several more miles in silence when Alex abruptly spoke up. "Are you hungry?"

Until that moment she had completely forgotten about her stomach, what with all the other loose ends of limb and life and libido with which to contend. But now she couldn't help but admit to an urgent gnawing within. "Yes," she declared.

"If we make a detour a few miles up, there's a great truck stop—if you don't mind a few leers. What do you feel like?" Alex asked.

"What do you feel like?"

"No, you first. I took the initiative to ask the question. You can assume some responsibility."

Cassandra felt this was reasonable enough. "Hamburger," she said reflectively.

"Nice," he commented, and added, "Fries."

"Chocolate malt," she ventured with enthusiasm.

He matched her with, "Onion rings."

"Steak sandwich," she rang out. There was the potential for a gastronomic orgy. This was something she could really get into. At last they had a neutral, common ground of interest—gluttony.

"Baked potato." But it was tentative.

"You aren't certain?" she asked. "I mean, I detected a less than wholehearted commitment to the idea of a spud."

"I don't know . . . I've got to think about it. Potato, potato . . ." A moment was taken for deep reflection, then he declared, "Butter, sour cream, chives, bacon bits . . . like that." And it was emphatic.

"Chocolate malt."

"You said that," he corrected.

"I want another one."

"Okay, if you're loosening the standards . . . sex," he said.

"Go to hell."

"Why? If you get two chocolate malts, why can't I—"

"I am not a snack," she said tightly. Clearly the ride that had begun so well was heading downhill, so to speak.

"Fine. Be the main course, then."

"We're running low on gas," she said, glad to move the conversation to something as safe and basic as being stranded in the desert at night.

Alex leaned over—that is, bound stiff as a board, he slanted himself to the side—and examined the reading on the gauge. "No, not really," he said, slanting himself back to an upright position.

"What do you mean, not really?" Cassandra retorted. "Very clearly it says almost empty."

"That doesn't mean anything. That's a conventional gauge. This isn't a conventional machine under the hood.

When it gets down to that spot, you've got another two, three hundred miles. At least."

"No car goes two or three hundred *more* miles."

Alex smiled at her. "This isn't any ordinary car. People are trying to kill me for it, if you recall."

"So this heap gets a million miles a gallon, huh?"

"Not quite. But a gallon'll take you on a long ride."

"Just so it gets you home." Cassandra put her foot down on the gas and sped ahead.

The road they traveled was dark, the moon hidden behind one of the mountain passes. Suddenly a flash of light appeared in the rearview mirror. Cassandra glanced back, but the vehicle was no longer in sight.

"Did you see that?" she asked.

Alex was looking out his window. "The light?"

"The light."

"Yeah."

"And?"

"Probably a truck or car. Some tanked-up old guy going home to his spread in the outback after a night of carousing."

"But it was there, and then it was gone."

"He made a turn, is all."

"No. The lights were there, and then they weren't. Just like that."

"Old ghosts. Lots of sightings of old ghosts on these roads. Ever hear of the Lost Dutchman?"

"He was on the ocean. In a boat. That means he's a couple of hundred miles off course, sailing in sand."

"This was his cousin. Drives an old jeep. Just drives and drives and drives and drives and—"

"Let me guess...he drives."

"Smart lady."

"Could anyone be following us?" Cassandra asked, her eyes darting again to the rearview mirror. "And don't be cute for once. Just straight out, yes or no."

"Maybe. Yeah, they might be."

She shook her head. "You're really impossible, you know? You got me into this damn mess, and when I try to deal with it in a reasonable manner, you act like it's just some big game or something. There might be killers out there, waiting—"

"To blast holes through both our skulls," Alex finished wearily. "Not to worry. They've got to be a little bit cool. Sure, they want me out of the picture, and they also want to have the car out of the scene. But I don't think they're necessarily going to destroy the engine. Eventually they could turn a nice profit on it themselves. So they aren't going to riddle the whole car full of holes, not even to do me in."

"And me. Don't overlook that small item while you're running down your list of probabilities."

"And you. They wouldn't exactly relish the idea of having a witness to the execution, would they?"

"Somehow I don't think so," Cassandra replied glumly.

"Thing of it is, I'm sure they'd like nothing better than to wipe both of us off the planet in one nice round of fire. But they can't. They'd run the risk of doing some sort of irreparable damage to the engine. It's a marvel—but a complicated marvel. It's totally conceivable that someone can figure it out once they have the model to themselves, but since it's new and revolutionary—as they say in the soap ads—they've got to have it intact or they're never going to duplicate it." He looked at her, and with a happy note to his voice said, "So I don't really think we need to worry about going up in flames tonight."

"Oh, thanks," Cassandra said. "That makes me feel a whole lot better."

"My pleasure. Of course," Alex said, thinking aloud, "they also have to get rid of Gordo and Charlie. But they're big enough targets. I don't think they're going to have too much trouble in doing the old Bomb and Charlie in." He paused. "Poor Jerry certainly didn't stand much of a chance against the bastards."

His voice had trailed off slightly. It was real emotion Cassandra heard coming through. There wasn't a trace of bravado in the last sentence. Cassandra cursed him. He was being wonderful again, downright human, connecting with her heart. The rat. She needed that underlying sensitivity like she needed the bullet through her head.

It was quiet again.

Cassandra could feel his thoughts as if they were tangible objects. Bleeding through the stillness, they were despairing and frightened; the mind products of a lonely man who wasn't accustomed to sharing his feelings.

"Those guys are like family to you, aren't they?" Cassandra ventured.

"Business partners," he mumbled. He shifted his weight against the seat. "So," Alex said, obviously dissembling, "what do you think of it?" He waved his arm, taking in the automobile.

"It needs new upholstery."

"The engine."

"The engine goes. What can I tell you? I don't know about engines."

"Would you like to?"

"No."

"Oh," he said. They drove along for a while in more silence, and then he asked, "What about you? Any family?"

This was the first semblance of real conversation they had ever had. It didn't contain any hint of death or mayhem. It wasn't about food. It wasn't even about sex. She didn't know how to respond. All her energy had been expended in defending herself from involvement with him. Now it seemed impossible to unlock the gates to carry on in a civilized manner. She simply didn't want to get any closer to him. It was too tricky. Pools that looked innocent sometimes contained quicksand.

So she said, "A mother. A brother. In Iowa."

"Your father?"

"Dad passed away. Three years ago."

He gave no comment, and Cassandra figured that she'd let the conversation drop naturally rather than try to knock herself out being polite by asking him questions about his own life, just to be cut off by him again. He didn't like to get close, that much was for certain. And yet he made attempts now and then to form some kind of a relationship. It was just difficult for her to figure out what kind he wanted. Certainly there was the sexual aspect; he was straightforward enough about that! But in the shack he had let her into his heart, too. It might have been just for a visit, but she could tell it was a warm place with comfortable furniture—a place all set up to be lived in, but for the occupants. She would have liked to have attributed his general sense of emotional distance to being hunted down by a string of unknown killers, but she couldn't. There was more to it than that. Maybe Alex Montana had been hurt badly. Maybe someone had once lived in that heart with him, and then had left. Maybe once he had been a different man entirely. Maybe he didn't even cause the relationship to fall apart. Maybe, thought Cassandra, she was losing her marbles thinking so much. Not maybe: most likely that was the case—she was suffering from spilled marbles.

"For what it's worth to you," Alex said, "I don't find any of this amusing. Not the guys in the black van today. Not the lights that show up and then disappear. For what it's worth to you, I am not all that eager to leave before my time."

"That's a relief," Cassandra said, trying to lift him out of the gloom she heard in his voice.

"I'm going to stay alive long enough to see that Gordo and Big Charlie get a fair shake out of this deal."

"Altruism?"

"Too grand," Alex said. "More being stubborn than anything else. I don't much care for anyone shoving me around. I didn't take it from the bulls—except for that big black one—and I'm sure as hell not going to take it from a gaggle of two-footed snakes with guns."

"Yup," Cassandra said, "you're a real hard case all right. Taking care of Gordo and Charlie doesn't enter into the picture at all."

He was quiet for a moment. "They're kind of like kids, you know? I don't know," he said, sighing, "sometimes I feel like I'm their father, and it's up to me to make things come out right for them. Like they've been disappointed by life for so long, if I don't do it for them..." He let it go at that.

"And you?" Cassandra asked, intrigued now, in spite of herself, that he was opening up. "How's life been for you?"

"Oh, I've had things pretty good. All in all."

"Getting stomped on by bulls is pretty good?" Cassandra asked, and laughed.

"Better than getting kicked in the teeth by the two-legged variety of critter." He laughed, too.

A darker note had crept into the delivery, which Cassandra was certain had been meant to be taken as light fluff, throwaway information. For a while there was no talk between them. Only the peculiar gurgling sound of the engine filled the atmosphere. It was a strange sound. He was a strange man. She would be glad when she wouldn't have to think about him anymore.

There was a flash of light behind them again. Cassandra caught the beam in her rearview mirror. Alex caught it in his side mirror. The light didn't disappear this time. It was getting brighter, and it was coming up fast on their tail.

Chapter Six

Cassandra...?" Alex had twisted his body around and was staring out the back window. Cassandra didn't like the way his brow was furrowed. She hoped it was due to eye strain and not worry.

"What?" Her voice sounded very small next to the ruckus being made by her heart. It was beating out a wild tattoo. She really didn't want to know "what." She wanted to be home, in bed, asleep, dreaming of a great shoe sale, or her prince.

"Have you ever watched one of those Grand Prix races?"

"In person?"

"On television, in person..."

"Television." The lights behind them were becoming larger, which meant closer.

"How'd you like them?"

"They go very, very fast, Alex." And the direction of this conversation was getting to be very, very bad. She moved her attention from the road and the mirror to look across at him. "Sometimes the drivers who are professionals, Alex, lose control of the cars and crash and die."

"Umm," Alex said, still watching out the back. "It's damn dangerous business, speed like that."

"Yes, it certainly is," Cassandra said. The sense of dread, which had begun with the first glint of light in the rearview mirror, was growing with each word they exchanged.

"But," he said, turning around and refastening his seat belt, "it sure as hell beats being run off the road by some dudes who want to do you in." He gave the metal cinch a hardy tug. It held.

"I, uh, get the feeling you're trying to tell me something. Could I be right about that?" The headlights were gaining on them. When she looked, the glare made her squint. The light was sharp and flat and lethal, reminding her of one of those martial arts exhibitions done with swords, where the blades would flash as they sliced through the air.

"You *are* perceptive. It seems that . . . oh, yeah . . . here we are."

Alex didn't have to tell her. At that instant the headlights were all but in their back seat. Like a monster with glowing eyes, the vehicle behind them lunged forward and bumped their rear end.

There was a crunching sound as one of the taillights was eliminated. Cassandra's hands slipped off the steering wheel. "Alex!" The car flew off crazily at an angle.

Alex reached across and grabbed the wheel, righting the car back to its path before it could spin out of control. Cassandra's hands again clamped around the wheel. Her knuckles were white. "God..." she said. "Alex, they're maniacs."

The pursuers attacked again from the back.

"Just killers," he said.

This time they smashed the other side. Another crunch and clatter sounded. The second taillight was extinguished. They were being dismantled piece by piece. Soon, Cassandra figured, she would be sitting on a seat, with nothing around her but the desert night.

Her entire body was frozen, her mind exclusively engaged with the white line running down the middle of the road. It seemed to fill her mind, that line, to occupy her entire attention. In the periphery of her consciousness, she could hear Alex saying, "Okay, babe, punch it. Punch it, Cassandra! Now!"

And she did. Somehow.

Tears were running down her face, hot, sticky, copious tears. They fell across her lip and trickled down her chin.

The pursuing car was at their side now, bumping against them. It was the black van. From the corner of her eye, Cassandra saw two hollow eyes set in a white expanse of flesh, staring at her. Then she realized it wasn't just a white expanse of flesh. She was looking at what had to be bandages. Gauze was wrapped around the head of their assailant.

"It's them," she said. "Alex, it's them...the ones from the afternoon."

"The very ones."

"He's got his head all taped up."

"They must have been at the hospital," he said.

"We're going to die, aren't we?" she said. "This is how it's going to happen. You never think it's really going to happen. You read about it happening to other people, and it doesn't seem real, and you never think that something

like that could happen to you. But it's going to happen."
The words ran on, one syllable into another, nonstop.

"Cassandra, you don't know how sorry I am—"

"I know you didn't mean for things to get so out of control," she said, at the same time wondering where all this generosity was coming from. It was downright incongruous, considering the history of their relationship.

"—that you're the one driving."

"I don't mind, Alex."

"I do. You're such a lousy driver, Cassandra."

Her eyes narrowed. She would have given him a totally scathing look, filled with hatred, but she couldn't take her eyes off the road. They were traveling too fast, and just trying to stay on course was using up most of her energy.

It made her furious, that statement. He was starting up with her again. In the company of death, he still had time to be a pain in the ass!

She was a fabulous driver! If there was one thing on this whole earth that she did superbly, at which she was an absolute virtuosa, it was driving.

"If we die," she said between clenched teeth, "it is not going to be tonight. It is not going to be in this car. It is not going to be because those creeps in that black van catch us, either."

The van had moved up in front of them, a gleaming force of malevolent metal.

"There!" Cassandra gave a whoop. "They're leaving! They're clearing out, Alex!" She understood the saying "an explosion of joy."

"Uh, wrong, baby."

Thirty feet ahead, the van had fishtailed to a stop. It was positioned at a slant, blocking the road.

Cassandra reduced her speed, her mind spinning in faster circles than her tires as she tried to decide what to do.

"I think that's a hint for us to stop," Alex said.

"Tough," Cassandra said. "I want a malt. And I want it now. Murdering us will just have to wait."

With that declaration, she floored the gas pedal, and the car lifted into another gear, the force of acceleration jerking their heads back. "Ha!" she cried, using the martial arts inflection taught to her by Og. "Hai!"

"Holy smokes..." Alex said as they hurtled straight for the van.

Another few feet and they'd be at the point of impact. All at once, Cassandra felt the earth at rest. The spinning of her mind stopped. Serenity enveloped her. Everything was amazingly clear, the world and all her senses in focus.

Before them, the doors of the van flew open, and three men jumped out, rolling and flailing their arms around as if on fire.

Cassandra laughed, and at the last minute turned the wheel sharply. Their vehicle flew off the road, becoming airborne for a moment as they sailed over a shallow rut off the shoulder of the road and finally landed on level earth. She was still clearheaded, the adrenaline pumping like crazy through her body, a sense of exhilaration filling every cell. She was electric, and at the same time, she was completely serene.

"This is fun!" she cried out.

"I don't mean to dim your enthusiasm for flying, Cassandra, but this engine was built for the earth."

"What, you don't like traveling at Mach Two? Great engine, Montana. Really great. You're going to really do yourself proud when you show up at the Sports Arena."

"Oddly, it's not the thugs I'm so worried about anymore...."

Cassandra heard, or imagined she heard, the engine's pulse, as if beneath the hood was a giant heart, courageous and pure and indefatigable.

The car was zipping through the night, eating up the desert floor. The moon was visible again, shining through a break between mountains. Cacti were blue in the moonlight. A jack rabbit, bounding for its life across her path, was silver. They hit a rut in the earth, flew for an instant, then thumped down to packed earth.

"Uhh..." Alex groaned.

In her euphoria over having outrun the killers, she had all but forgotten Alex's condition. The sound of pain reminded her of the reality of the situation. It wasn't so much fun anymore. The pleasurable current coursing through her body shut down.

Again her heart began its terrified pattern of thumping exclamations. She must be mad, she reasoned. Absolutely bonkers. She started to slow, all strength gone from her body, her mind mush.

"Don't slow down," Alex said. "But do get back on the road."

Like an automaton, she did as she was told.

"Now," Alex continued, "keep going at just this speed, and when you come to the next sign, turn right. There's no sign, just a road. We're going to cut across the desert and pick up the highway."

"Alex..." she said, "they're coming again!"

And so they were.

This time she did exactly as she was told. She drove like an arrow that Alex aimed, taking each curve as he instructed, raising or lowering the speed as he indicated. It may have taken ten miles or ten minutes or ten years, but the lights were suddenly gone from behind them.

They continued to drive in silence. She didn't know where, didn't care much, either. She had no feeling left; everything had been drained out of her in direct proportion to the former elation she had experienced.

When they passed a sign welcoming them to Arizona, even that didn't seem strange. If a Martian had landed on her hood, it would have just been another event in her messed-up life, and she would have kept driving.

Twenty minutes after they had passed the sign, they came into a patch of lights. A small town rose twinkling out of the desert.

"Slow down," Alex said.

She did.

"Pull in there," Alex ordered.

Cassandra turned the wheel and cruised into a parking lot. A glowing green neon cactus had Vacancy bannered across its front. "Alex, this is a motel," Cassandra said.

"That's what it is, all right. Park over there by the office."

Cassandra did as she was told, pulling into a slot by a real cactus. "I don't think I want to—"

"Cassandra, I'm too tired to—" he shook his head, then looked away "—do anything but sleep. I certainly don't have the stuff it takes to argue with you now. So," he said with a yawn, and ran his hand over his face, "you can please yourself. You can get your own room. You can sleep out here. You can stay in a room with me and save a couple of bucks."

Cassandra considered the options. "I want a hamburger," she said.

"Fine. Go to it. There's probably an all-night burger joint open somewhere on this main drag." With that, he removed the keys from the ignition, got out of the car and dragged himself over to the office door. A minute or two later he came out again and shuffled painfully back to her side of the door.

He tapped on her window and showed her the room key. "Two beds," he said, his voice muffled through the glass. She stared back at him, thinking and not thinking. It was so hard to make any kind of decision. She definitely wanted a hamburger, but it was going to be hard to get that message across to her body. Body and mind seemed to be disconnected.

Alex was apparently waiting for her to do something, or to say something. She saw him as if she were viewing a fish through a glass tank. Or perhaps it was she who was the fish and he was viewing her. It was hard to tell about that, too. Finally he gave up trying to get some sort of response from her and marched away. Through the glass she could hear the crunch-crunch of his steps on the gravel.

He arrived in front of a pastel pink door whose front was sun-blasted through to the wood in places. There were three plastic flowers planted in more gravel by the door. Red scalloped bricks formed a border between the gravel flower bed and the gravel drive.

Cassandra watched as he opened the door. He stepped inside. The lights went on. The door remained open. She sat there for two or three minutes, possibly longer. Then one of those inexplicable impulses propelled her out of the car, and she, too, crunched her way to the open motel door. She looked in. Alex was nowhere to be seen. Her heart constricted; in an instant, her mouth had become cottony. Then she heard water running from behind the bathroom door and relaxed.

Still held by indecision on the doorstep, looking into the room, Cassandra shivered. The night had turned cool. It was, after all, February; the desert sun might be pleasant during the daylight hours, but at night the moon drank what warmth there had been. Inside, the beds looked inviting. There was also the matter of her stomach. She did not know how Alex managed, but her stomach was giving her pains, and waves of nausea washed through her at frequent intervals. She was almost too weak and disoriented to reason things out. It was possible, she thought wildly, that she would never decide anything and that she would eventually die right there on the stoop of a pink stucco motel in Arizona. With supreme effort, she pulled herself together long enough to organize her situation into three parts, the better to deal with them in a rational manner. She was tired, she was hungry and she was cold. In her mind she saw the small list. There was comfort in clarity. It made her life almost real again.

So, she considered, reviewing her list, she had better sleep, get something to eat and keep warm. But, in reverse order.

Stepping into the motel room, she snatched the cotton bedspread from one of the twin mattresses, and wrapped it around her shoulders. Her wallet had a twenty-dollar bill in it, which was certainly enough for a hamburger or two or three and a chocolate malt.

She would have driven, but Alex had taken the keys and apparently had them locked up with him in the bathroom, where the water was still going full blast. Never mind, she would walk. The town was small; within half a mile, there was bound to be something. A check with the office told her as much.

A half hour later she was back at the motel. This time the door was closed, and she had to beat on it for a while until Alex came.

He was wearing boxer shorts when he opened the door. His eyes were puffed and red, his hair mussed. He had been sleeping.

"Where were you?" he asked, leaving her to shut the door as he staggered back to his bed.

"Chow," she said, and threw a bag with a hamburger and fries on his mattress.

Alex sat on the edge of the bed. Instead of breaking into the feast she had provided he just stared at the white bag.

"You aren't going to eat?" she asked, peeved at his lack of appreciation for her good deed. Then she asked, "Weren't you worried about me?" It was this that truly annoyed her, not his lack of interest in the fries, but that he had fallen asleep while she might have been abducted. Or worse.

He looked up at her, his eyes slightly unfocused as if seeing her through a long tunnel. Or maybe it was she who was seeing him through a long tunnel. Her eyes seemed to be bugging out of her head from fatigue, and now her stomach felt even worse than from the hunger pains. The burger might have been a brick lying on the bottom of her stomach, and she felt as if even her vocal cords were bruised from stuffing too many fries down at once.

"I'm not hungry anymore," Alex said at last. "Thanks, though." He fell back onto the bed, his bandages looking like a gun holster, taped as they were around his shoulder and chest.

Cassandra waited. Had he heard the second question?

"Alex?"

"Ummm..." His eyes had closed, and his breathing was already taking on the rhythm of sleep.

"Alex! Weren't you even wondering what had happened to me?"

"Ummm..."

"Well, then," she said, "how could you have fallen asleep?"

"Ummm..."

She came around to the side of the bed and shook him awake. "Alex, maybe I was being murdered out there!"

His eyelids fluttered open. "Cassandra...if you don't shut up, I'm going to kill you myself." His eyes closed again.

Cassandra gave him a shove. "Let me tell you something!" She was so angry she was gasping. She was so furious her voice was cracking. She even began to sob, but she was going to say what she was going to say.

Alex's eyes were open again, and alert, even wary. He had every right to be alarmed. She was on the verge of...of something...

"I...I am tired of taking care of you. I am sick of it! I took care of Og. And he ran out on me. And I took care of you today, and then...when I needed someone to worry about me...you...you fell asleep! And I don't like it...I don't think it's fair. You didn't have to even do anything. Just...be worried." She was sobbing so hard she could barely stand. "I...I..." Her shoulders heaved and her chest caved inward as she brought her hands over her face. Shame washed over her. She was behaving like a maniac, like a baby, like a stupid fool.

"Oh...God..." she sobbed, and rushed into the bathroom, slamming the door after her. Leaning over the sink, she clutched the white porcelain as if it were a life raft that could save her from drowning in humiliation.

She didn't hear him come in behind her, and when his hands came softly over her shoulders, she jumped and whirled around, her first instinct to lash out protectively, her second, upon seeing Alex, to hide her face. She attempted to bolt, but he caught her. "Leave me be!" she cried.

"Cassandra!" he said, and pulled her roughly against him before she could escape.

"Just leave me alone. I've made a complete spectacle of myself, and if you have any sense of decency in you, you'll just let me get over this."

"I have no sense of decency in me," Alex said, and tried to lift her into his arms. But he couldn't. He was taped too tightly. He grimaced from the pain. "Come on," he said, and with an unexpectedly sharp jerk, pulled her back into the bedroom. He sat her down on his bed. Immediately a protest rose from her.

"Just shut up," he said as he began to undress her.

It wasn't an erotic scene. It was a methodical, business-like affair, in which each item was removed in due course. When she was down to her underwear, Alex turned and pulled back the covers of her bed. He even plumped her pillow. "Okay," he said, facing her once again, "get in there."

Obediently she moved across the small aisle separating the two beds and climbed into her bed. He covered her in the sheet and blanket before she could do it for herself. Her head throbbed, and her eyes were like heavy ball bearings in her skull as she looked up at him.

"Go to sleep," he said. "You're just overtired." Their eyes met and held. "Cassandra . . . it wasn't that I didn't care about what happened to you."

"Then what was it?"

"It was . . ."

"Fatigue . . ." she said, and turned her face into the pillow.

Almost angrily, he reached down and pulled her jaw back to face him. "No," he said. "No, it wasn't fatigue. It was . . ." Again he stopped. "Something else."

Chapter Seven

Alex turned off the light, then slipped into his own bed and pulled the covers to his chin. In vain he waited for sleep to overtake him. He turned on his side and tried to slow his whirling mind. Fifteen minutes passed, then twenty, and still the restlessness persisted.

In the dark he could hear the soft, regular brush of Cassandra's breath against the air.

Only moments before she had been choking on emotion, hardly able to stand. Her blue eyes had burned with fury at him, and her voice had been an assault, each letter of every word a stone against his conscience. Now the anguish was lost in the blessed relief of sleep. Lucky Cassandra.

She had been right, of course; that was the pity of it, the irony of it, maybe even the beauty of it, Alex reflected. It proved—as his mother used to claim—that you couldn't run away from the truth.

Well, he had sure given evasion of that principle a good shot over the years; anyone would grant him that. What a race it had been: he, fleet of feeling, truth always a breath behind, and never winded. But here it was again, the truth cornering him when it was least expected—or wanted—on the scene, making its entrance in a run-down motel in a jerkwater Arizona town in the middle of the desert. There just didn't seem to be a crack anymore through which a fellow might escape.

"Pride cometh before the fall," was another thing his mother had been fond of repeating.

"Well, if you don't have enough guts to go after something, Mom, then you're going to be down on your hands and knees groveling around to make ends meet anyway. So why not try?" he'd argued.

His mother had told him why.

She told him that his dad had tried to be more than he was, had borrowed—without her knowledge—a heap of money from a few sources, none of which was the bank, which had better sense than to loan him a cent, and had—naturally—failed in his scheme.

For the longest while Alex could not understand why his father remained, year after year, placidly taking his mother's abuse. Alex had loved his mother, but his own relationship was different. On Alex she lavished her attentions. Her dreams for him knew no bounds. Still, Alex could separate himself enough from the total family drama to see that no man in his right mind would find anything worthwhile in such a negative relationship. During Alex's puberty, the question of his father's steadfast devotion troubled Alex far more than the mysteries of female anatomy and psyche.

One would have thought it reasonable that another man burdened by such a harpy of a wife, not to mention the ill will of the creditors he had failed, and having no future possibility of making anything of himself, would have taken the next bus out of town.

Well, his father hadn't taken that option. Or perhaps in a sense he had, but it wasn't a physical deed. In time Alex came to understand that emotionally his father had checked out of the scene.

Alex could remember coming home to their little house after school and finding his father sitting on the sofa, staring off into space. On other days he might find his father outside, sitting on one of the old cars he had collected to restore but never did. His father would be quietly looking inward at some scene none of them could ever fathom, although on several occasions Alex had attempted to discuss the content of the private screening. It was baffling. What could his father think of for such long stretches?

Unlike his mother, Alex did not hold to the belief that his father was crazy, or deliberately being cruel by keeping them out of his life. Alex's own opinion was that his father had simply found another world to inhabit and that this better place just so happened to be within.

Although his father's failure as a provider was the principal issue in their family's life, his father said little about the matter. He offered no defense whatsoever. Actually it wasn't just one great failure that placed in his mother's litany of complaints. There were a whole string of minor disappointments to review as well, all connected to his father's efforts to make more money. Even Alex had to admit his mother had some grounds for complaint. Among other schemes his father had at one time or another embarked upon, there was the chicken ranch fiasco. This was a natural segue into the mink ranch business, which led in turn to mail-order mink oil facial rejuvenation, which eventually evolved into the great and final Miracle Mile epoch of defeat and humiliation.

This was his father's last stand—this gasoline-stretching product, which he had come across one dark day in Seattle, Washington, while visiting his brother. Apparently his brother had gone in on the product himself, but in a minor way. It was a pyramid-structured enterprise: each distributor got a percentage of sales from every new distributor he brought into the fold beneath him.

In a large convention hall, Alex's father had listened to the spiel of the salesman from the Detroit Miracle Mile corporate headquarters. The speaker had been ablaze with passion for the product, which he had likened in importance to the invention of the wheel. A man could go three times farther on a gallon of gasoline merely by adding a cup of Miracle Mile Liquid to his tank after every fill-up at the station. Why—Alex's father was later to claim with the same religious fervor—Miracle Mile could be sold everywhere! The outlets for this boon to mankind were endless, inexhaustible: gas stations and convenience stores along highways were targets, and department stores, neighbors—who would themselves beg to become distributors—and even the military would line up to make its purchase. Not only was the product going to make the seller money, but it was going to provide a service to mankind that was beyond any monetary value—ecology would be benefited.

Alex remembered the day the cartons arrived. There were about fifty of the large brown boxes. They seemed to take up the entire backyard when they were unloaded. They came in a large truck that read Shep Brothers—One-Way Hauls. Alex also remembered wondering about the one-way haul logo. Later he was to find out that the flow of money related to the Miracle Mile Enterprise went only one way—to Miracle Mile in Detroit.

His father set out immediately to recoup his investment. He brought the bottles around the neighborhood first, talking up a good storm about the benefits and, either out of kindness or general belief, he sold about ten half-gallon bottles worth of the product. It came as a crushing blow when some of his customers demanded their money-back guarantee be enforced. The others probably were too embarrassed to bother with righting the wrong, and wrote off the twenty-dollar loss to neighborliness.

The thing of it was, the product simply didn't work. At the convention there had been small toy cars exhibited on the stage, cars that were filled with regular gasoline except for one group to which the product had been added. The cars were set off on separate little tracks and left to run throughout the program as the salesman gave his spiel. Alex's father related how the tension mounted something fierce toward the latter part of the program as more and more of the straight gasoline-powered cars sputtered and died to a cold stop, while the Miracle-Mile-augmented cars whizzed along their course.

That's what made it all so incredible, said Alex's father. He had seen the product work with his very own eyes!

At first, when the bottles were returned, he called the corporate headquarters and was told the problem was undoubtedly because the people were using a low-grade fuel that detracted from the Miracle Mile special formula. Elated, Alex's father relayed the information to his customers. No one, however, wanted anything more to do with Miracle Mile. Some neighbors felt the same way about Alex's father. All in all, it was a tense time socially.

Saddened but not defeated, Alex's father continued blindly on the sales course set by the corporate staff of

Miracle Mile, disappearing into the state for three weeks to peddle his bottles. By the time he came back, a notice had been sent by the state district attorney to cease and desist sale of the product Miracle Mile. In essence, the government considered the boon to mankind as no more than a scam.

Still a believer, Alex's father called Detroit. The telephone number was no longer in operation. Miracle Mile had simply vanished into thin air, along with his father's money and dreams.

The worst of it was that his father had borrowed money from several of his boyhood friends, whom he had convinced of the product's worthiness.

So, from the time Alex was eleven until he graduated from high school and went away to college, he had lived beneath the dark cloud of the "Miracle Mile mess." An atomic cloud could not have caused more grief; and even such a cloud as that had the grace to move on. But the Miracle Mile mess remained with the family, became, in fact, like another member of the house, so often was it mentioned in reference to what could or could not be done because of "It."

And for years Alex watched his father tune the whole thing out.

There was one occasion, however, when his father emerged as a faint shadow of the man he had once been. It occurred on the day Alex left to attend college in Portland. His father left the sofa and emerged from Inner Land long enough to walk out to the car.

Alex would remember the conversation the rest of his life.

"I guess you think I've gone nuts," his father had said.

"No, Dad. I don't think that."

"I have gone nuts, I guess."

"No, Dad. You just tried hard, and things went bad for you. I guess it hurt a lot, what happened. So you went inside."

His father's eyes glassed over, and Alex was afraid he was going to cry. He himself wanted to cry.

"I loved her," his father said.

At first Alex didn't know whom his father meant. It took him a while to figure it out. When he did he was stunned. "Mom?"

His father nodded. He looked off, this time not into himself, but beyond their property line. "It was for her. I wanted to show her how much I loved her. I wanted to do things, great things." He shook his head, and then he really was crying. Large, slow tears fell one after the other from both eyes.

"Oh, Dad...don't...please." Alex was beside himself. He didn't know what to do. He wanted to hug his father, to take care of him, as if his father were the kid. But it had been so long since they had touched, and he simply didn't know what the hell to do.

At the point when Alex thought he might break apart from the tension, it was his father who suddenly came through, rising to the occasion like the champ he had never quite been.

His father reached out and brushed Alex's cheek, as if it were he who were crying. "You do good now," his father said. "You make something good of yourself, just like your mama always wanted." His hazel eyes misted over then, and in them Alex could see a little scene being played back in which his father was a different man, successful and smiling, and his mother was hugging him, jumping around all happy.

"Damn," Alex said violently. "Why, Dad? Why'd you let everything fall apart? Why didn't you do anything?"

His father didn't hear him, though. His father was back in Inner Land. Alex was alone again, excluded.

Only now Alex knew what his father was seeing when he left the world the rest of them had to live in. His father was seeing what he wanted to see. Really, he hadn't ever left the family. He had just been with them the way he wanted them to be. He had retreated to a place inside where everything could be beautiful.

Alex left that day, with his mother behind his college career one hundred percent. He had gotten a scholarship to a private college, which had taken him because of his superior mechanical aptitude. It was a small, elite school, out of which a few world-class scientists had been hatched. The trustees were hungry to add names to the school's ranks of successes. They were betting on Alex.

Most of the students, however, weren't really scholars. They were the children of the West Coast wealthy, who would merely absorb the heirs to the family fortunes into their pre-made kingdoms when the time was right. The four-year program of undergraduate study was actually four years of political jockeying for social prestige, a prelude to what the rest of their lives would become.

Alex did well in his studies. He tried to fit in socially, but couldn't. When things became tough, he even tried to go "within," as his father did, but he didn't have his father's talents.

Then, having apparently inherited one of his father's "stupid genes," he made the fatal mistake of falling in love.

Her name was Sam—Samantha—Ellison. She came slinking into his life like a sleek cat of the most regal breeding. Like the Miracle Mile snake oil salesman, Sam captivated and enthralled and enslaved him beneath her green-eyed spell. And then she threw him away.

He was in his senior year, with one semester to go before he would graduate top of his class in mechanical engineering. Suddenly Alex found himself unable to think, unable to feel, unable ... period.

His few friends pointed out that his situation had been suffered by countless other jilted lovers since time immemorial. Being dumped was rough, but you lived through it. All it took was time.

But Alex didn't have time. He had only one semester, and all he could do was weep secretly during long walks in the woods and sleep when he should have been hitting the slide rule.

He failed two important tests.

But the failure grew in his eyes until it wasn't that he had blown a couple of tests—just two lousy tests during his entire college experience—but that he, like his father, was doomed to let himself and everyone else down.

Unlike his father, he didn't hang around on a sofa and retreat into another world. Maybe he would have had he been given that option. But all he had was one semester to trip out—or *in*, as in his dad's case—and then he'd have to find some other sofa to roost upon for the rest of his days. He even thought of returning home. He imagined himself and his father sitting side by side on their living room sofa, the living-unliving. The idea was cast aside.

He left college on a Monday morning when everyone was in class. He hitched a ride all the way to Texas, not knowing what he was going to do from hour to hour, let alone for the rest of his life, since he could barely keep a coherent thought in his mind.

The question of his immediate future was answered by providence when he landed a job taking care of a downed rodeo rider's ponies for a month. The job was just to earn some money to keep going east. But in that month he dis-

covered two uplifting pieces of information: he didn't have
to think to get up on a horse and fall down, and the women
who hung around these cowboys were several notches
down in class from Sam Ellison. That made the women
safe.

In spite of his devastating experience with romance, he
still needed women in his life. He liked women actually. He
liked to touch them and sleep with them and make them
laugh, and every now and then to buy them little things to
make them happy. But he was incapable of ever falling in
love again. Relationships evolved up to the point where he
felt safe. He only picked women whom he could dominate. He also picked women several degrees down in looks,
personality and class from the kind of women he really
wanted. He kept himself safe.

Tonight, however, in this rathole of a motel he had lost
his safety buffer. When he had come out of the shower and
found Cassandra gone, his heart had constricted to the
point that he had lost his breath for a moment. It was a
shock, that kind of feeling. He had only felt it once, and
that was the day Samantha had left the note for him in his
dorm mailbox. The note was Sam all the way, right down
to the neat dots and straight-crossed *t*'s: cold and efficient, Sam had told him they were finished.

He had read the note and, as if he had been hit in the
gut, he had doubled over. He had even screamed, as he
later recalled in shame. Or maybe a better word for it was
howled. He had howled like a wounded animal.

In a minor way those same emotions had filled him this
evening. He had come out of the shower expecting to see
spunky, argumentative Cassandra Burke waiting for him
in the room. Only Cassandra was gone. All those old
"Sam" feelings came back. A blackness had settled over
him, invading every cell of his body. All he could do was

slip into bed and try to breathe correctly. The next thing he knew he was asleep. And the next thing he knew, Cassandra was back and...

Alex raised himself slightly and looked across to where she lay in sound slumber.

A feeling of excruciating tenderness fell like a net over him. If Sam reminded him of a cold, assured feline, then this woman was a soft, furry cat, meant to cuddle and purr in the sunlight of some nice, safe window in some pretty home; but having no such place, this girl cat struggled to fend for herself. Well, she did a hell of a job of it, Alex admitted to himself, a smile touching his heart. But she would fit better in the warm sunlight.

"Cassandra?" he said.

She didn't answer him. He waited a minute, and when he was certain she was absolutely sound asleep, he sat up a little more so he could see her clearly and said, "I did care tonight about what happened to you. The fact is, baby, I cared so damn much I fell asleep because the thought of anything happening to you scared the living bejeebers out of me. Cassandra... once I loved someone... and it hurt. So much. It hurt more than you could possibly, ever, ever imagine. And I just don't think I could—"

Alex closed his eyes and sank back into his pillow.

If he could get that engine to market, it would make everything right again.

Chapter Eight

Sometime during the night he must have fallen asleep. When he awoke, Cassandra was out of bed and in the bathroom showering. The sound of the water, the feeling of another human in close proximity, made the morning hopeful. He had almost allowed himself to indulge in the fiction that she was "sharing his life," but that would have been stretching reality too thin.

Nevertheless, his spirits were lighter than they had been in a long time, and an added plus was simply that he was still alive. That alone was something.

He rose and was at the window, peering outside through a crack in the closed draperies, dressed only in his boxer shorts and swathed in bandages, when the bathroom door opened.

Turning, he saw Cassandra entering the room. A faint mist of steam trailed after her. His senses quickened at first sight of her. Her hair and body were wrapped in white towels. The shiny glow to her skin and the freshness of her soapy scent combined to further bolster his mood. It was startling, this visual purity, this vision of wholesomeness; and the contrast to this experience, in relation to his past morning-after encounters with women, was so acute he found himself momentarily disoriented. It was as if another facet of the world had suddenly opened up for him. His mind reeled in confusion. He might have been looking at a painting whose scene had grown edges beyond itself, with mountains and rolling hills and valleys and forests rising full-blown into view. The landscape took on entirely new possibilities and dimensions, unknown before.

More times than he wanted to recall he had risen in the morning to face a strange woman. Always a different woman, the eyes, nevertheless, seemed identical, as if they were all borrowed from the same facial bank. They were tired eyes, circled with blue hollows and ringed in dark smudges of disappointment.

Hours before, the women's bodies entwined with his, harsh truths had been swallowed by the shadows of the night. Pasty faces were rendered pink, courtesy of a bar's indirect lighting, and ravaged countenances could masquerade as mystery rather than misery.

But always there was the morning, with its attendant cruel blast of reality tearing at seams constructed entirely of moonlight. Stripped of illusion, complexions were more gray than cream; faded rouge a parody of yet another temporary romance dissolved with the sun's appearance.

He and whatever woman it was would stare across the mattress at each other, naked, deprived of their protective night skins. And sometimes there was that instant when they would connect with each other. Of course, it was never *the* connection, the right one, the communion of body and spirit they both had sought. Nevertheless, it was an absolutely real experience, and because of that, a miserable, crippling moment whenever it happened. They would know that lying there together they were still alone.

The truth was, he was no better than the women. No great prize package he. Rising, strutting off to shower, he would begin his patter, the automatic verbal extrication of the relationship.

What was she going to be doing today? As if he cared.

He was going to go to the . . . and then he would . . . very busy, busy man. Blah-blah-blah.

When he spoke on those occasions, each word would have the color and depth of cardboard, all the conviction of the wind promising to stay awhile.

The woman of the moment, of course, would answer in kind. They were professionals, practiced in the art of pretense.

Gone from both of them was the crooning liquid timbre of the previous evening's revelry. Each breath they exchanged radiated another empty night's dissipation. All they could do was slide away quickly, with as little apology as possible for not being able to be lasting and real for each other.

But on *this* morning there was Cassandra.

Nowhere was to be seen an empty liquor bottle. There was no ashtray piled high with lipstick-stained cigarette butts. Absent were the half-filled glasses of whatever liquid moral anesthetic might have been swilled before getting down to the business of eradicating loneliness by way of the flesh. Nor was there, on this morning, an urgent necessity to make quick escapes from the terrible reality mirrored in another's face.

None of this was present, because he and Cassandra had not indulged in the con game of love.

To Alex the morning and the moment were as clean and fresh as the woman standing before him.

"Hi," Cassandra said, and her voice had the crystalline ring of small chimes in a pure mountain clime.

He breathed in, expanding in joy. "Hi," he said casually.

It was impossible to tell what feelings were held behind her large blue eyes. He was suddenly desperate to know her: the width, the breadth, the depth, the entirety of her, as if his life depended upon whatever she felt. In greeting, her eyes had brushed him gently, then were quickly lowered, like the wings of a butterfly folding protectively in on its body. Alex moved slightly, changing his angle of vision. "Did you sleep well?" he asked, something ordinary to hide his anxiety.

He might have touched her rather than spoken. Her shoulders tensed slightly, and her eyes rose again to his face. Their blue burned into him. He felt stained by their color. "Yes, fine," she said.

He had to say something. "Good."

They might have been teenagers, shy and waiting for the other to give direction to the relationship.

"And you?" she asked.

He could barely keep from grinning. She was as nervous as he! "I might have. I can't remember." It was the truth. His mind had forgotten everything. His entire life had been submerged beneath the blue expanse of her glance. Something very close to what he could remember as being happiness was alive in him again.

"I'm sorry about last night," she said.

His mind continued to be stuck in its groove of delight. With supreme effort, he pushed himself to speak. "Oh...you mean..." His hand moved, sweeping away the issue. "Don't be."

He could not take his eyes from her. Out of long habit he continued to wait for her to dissolve into one of those women whose skins resembled ashen cinders and whose eyes would become crystal balls holding a lifetime of aborted hopes.

But Cassandra remained as she was.

She had the most beautiful shoulders, mottled with pink and white splotches from the hot water. It was lovely, each coloration a stroke of genius from a master artist's brush. She was lovely.

He wanted to hold her, to press her body into his, as if that sense of health and purity she embodied in her person could take away the years of rodeo-circuit dust he had rolled in, and heal the bruises inflicted by horse and steer and other human animals—Sam Ellison among them.

That was asking for a lot. Then again, he needed a lot.

"I guess I was really tired," she said. She moved to her bed, and holding the towel tight against the swell of her breast with one hand, used the other to search through her bed covers.

"Lost something?" he ventured, not really interested in the answer. He was bewitched, unable to take full command of himself. The woman filled his mind, and each sense was tuned to her being. Rip away the towel, and he could bury his face in her breasts, run his hands along her buttocks, press his palm between her—

"My blouse." Cassandra shook her head disparagingly.

"What?"

"I can't find it," she said, and then he remembered the question.

"Probably tangled up in there somewhere. Perhaps I can be of some assistance." Gallant to the end, he was. He began to cross the room.

"It's okay. I'll find it," she muttered, engrossed in her search.

With each step his desire increased. He would take her standing up, lying down, against the wall, but he would have her as he had never made love to a woman in his life.

By her side, as cool as ever, he trembled within. The smell of her body...

"It's in here," Cassandra said, half determined, half doubtful. "Somewhere."

"If you'll allow me." She stepped back slightly, holding on tightly to the terry cloth towel gathered at her bosom.

Alex noted that in her search for the missing blouse, the ends of the towel had come slightly apart. In his present state, the slight separation of fabric was an invitation to paradise. Swallowing, he engaged in an intense display of sheet shaking. His fingers could barely feel the fabric. His legs were almost nonexistent beneath him. The pulsing in his groin had become a roar through his body. She was only inches from him. Inches! The air between them crackled with his desire.

Suddenly the blouse flew upward, like a bird rooted from shrubs. Cassandra reached forward, clutching for the airborne item of clothing. At the same time, the towel disengaged from its tenuous fold over her breast, and the terry cloth slipped downward, landing on the floor.

He bent to get the towel. At the same instant, Cassandra gave a slight cry of dismayed surprise and dipped to retrieve the covering herself. The collision was inevitable. Their heads bumped on the trip down, and Cassandra fell back, off-balance.

"Sorry, sorry..." Alex said, automatically reaching to steady her. His fingers came around one smooth pink-and-white arm. His eyes were elsewhere. In the back of his mind was the notion that this was the time to turn away, not only to avert his gaze, but to change the entire course of what was bound to follow. There was still time....

But his eyes were on her fully exposed breasts, and they traveled slowly, of their own accord, to the flat surface of her stomach, and below to the tuft of silken gold. They were close, too close, kneeling opposite each other, as if in position for the exchange of some ancient, sacred vow. Trembling, he closed his eyes and breathed in. Time did not move. She did not move. They did not move.

"Touch me," he heard her whisper.

At first he thought he had imagined the words. They were a manifestation of his overheated mind.

"Alex..." the voice said again, the yearning an echo of his own desire.

His eyes opened. Disbelievingly he looked into her face.

She must have understood. Taking his hand, she placed it first against her lips and kissed the back, then turned it over and flicked the palm lightly with her tongue.

It was all dreamlike, but not a sailor's dream of sex; this was something else entirely. This was the fantasy of his youth, before he was aware of the duplicity of the female species; before he had succumbed to maintaining his end of the sociological ritual that said men were to feel nothing but the animal thrill of passion. Once, long ago, before the outside world had invaded his sensibilities, he had dreamed of ladies with long silken skeins of hair, with voices like lutes, and bodies that melted and molded into his own flesh. Once or twice, long ago, he had dreamed of love.

And now, now...with this woman he was young again, and for a while it was long ago when fairy tales were possible.

He moved slowly closer, his body now a flow of continuous love. Their lips brushed, her mouth opening to his. His hunger for her was contained savagery, and there was in his self-imposed abstinence a thrill to the denial. On this razor's edge of violent passion, he experienced his desire fully, reveled in the taste and touch of her as his hand came around a breast, the other stroking her back, her neck, his finger sliding along the curve of her cheekbone.

Cassandra's breath had grown deep, and her shoulders shivered, heaving slightly as his finger toyed with the tip of her breast. An impression of silvery birch leaves, shuddering in a soft spring breeze drifted like a cloud through the landscape of his fevered mind. Layers upon layers of sensation swirled through his body—heat mingling with ice-cold; the romantic with the profane, carnal drive of a man roused to his peak; the soft yielding earth of a spring day, with the brittle ground of a winter's experience; the mundane pleasures of the world hitting hard against heaven's gate. It was a portal, God help him, through which he would enter soon . . . soon . . .

Her fingers were bursts of flame on his skin. Her mouth was dissolving him.

It was all he could do not to toss her to the floor and conquer her, to give vent to what he truly felt he had become: a madman, with no boundaries to his raging lust.

There was that element, and then . . . there was the other, the flickering pastel dream of his youth, to love . . . to join completely . . . that best part of himself with that best part of her. There had never been a "her" in his life. Once he had tried to fit Samantha into the role, but that had only been his desperate delusion. *She* had never appeared. Until now. And now he held her.

"Love me . . ." he said, his mouth hungry, but his heart even more famished, ready to devour her.

Slipping slowly down, Cassandra lay on the floor, her arms outstretched for him to join her. The bed was forgotten, the world faded into another realm. The only space that existed was the territory that lay in the eyes of the other. Nothing, nothing, made any difference to him but the amazing goddess who had entered his life two days ago. Against the floor, her fair damp hair lay like a burst of starlight around a face of such exquisite perfection that it pained him with sweet sorrow to look upon it.

"Alex...Alex," she said with a small smile and a quick intake of breath as he began to lower himself over her. Pressed against his own hardened form, her thighs were soft and round, rousing in him a tempestuous yearning to possess...to dominate. The words circled in him, hoops of sounds becoming sensations in the pit of his stomach, contracting his abdomen, tightening the muscles of his buttocks. Fire rushed in him. A path of molten liquid surged, stiffening him, making him hold still, trembling...fighting against his own need.

Cassandra felt for him, and with his eyes closed, he allowed himself to feel, to drift in sensation, then to retreat for fear of the bliss ending too soon.

"Please..." she said. "Alex...now."

Her mouth was against his ear, and she urged him to take her, telling him each desire, and no longer was she an unreachable goddess, and no longer was he holding to his youthful dream. He was a man and she was a woman, and in the connection of their flesh he entered, merging into a new reality of their mutual creation.

She cried out, her body arched like a bow against him.

"Cassandra...my love...at last, my love..." And Alex was moving with her, in unison, completely connected to each breath and each pulse of her heart and each contraction of every muscle. In her body, he was in her experience: filling her with himself, she became a part of him.

"Alex..." she sighed, drifting down slowly afterward. "Alex..." she breathed, her hands smooth and soft on his back. "Alex..."

They lay like that for a long time, their heartbeats eventually becoming separate again, and the cold room insinuating itself into a new state of reality.

Time had moved ahead. Thoughts and possibilities began to crowd the room, filling empty spaces that had allowed for the dreams to dance.

Her first movement came as a strident shock against his state of serenity. She turned her head sharply to the side.

He said nothing at first, merely tried to observe her from the corner of his eye. He waited in dread, suspecting that the moment of truth would not be long in coming. A sadness overwhelmed him, then a rage began to make slow progress through his body, climbing until it became too great and shattered into despair born of knowledge.

What they had shared was not real.

He wanted it to be real.

But she knew, and he knew, that what had just occurred between them was a product of imagination and circumstance.

"Damn," he said, his eyes closing. She was real, he was real, but what they had together was not real.

Cassandra sighed in response. She understood. He had spoken for her—for them. In one word all was conveyed.

Stirring slightly beneath him, she made a polite gesture of her wish to rise.

This was a different version of the morning after. Tricked again. God! He wanted to claw at the air!

For a moment they were still connected. His leg was over hers, his body slightly to the side, one arm slung across her breast. He trailed a hand lightly over her skin, reluctant to release their physical connection, and hating himself for that weakness. At last he allowed her the freedom to go.

Cassandra lifted herself off the floor, sitting in a huddled position, arms wrapped around her legs for a moment. She spoke into her knees, not even looking at him. "I'm sorry," she said.

"You're sorry," he repeated, his voice flat.

"Yes. I don't know how that happened."

"How it happened," he echoed. He felt in a daze, half in that magical world of loving they had shared, not yet able to merge with the pulse of the old reality in which he walked alone. Yet, even so, he rose to the occasion. A hard swallow, a tightening of the heart muscle, and he was able to summon the correct tone of superficiality to match the amorous fling. "So, it happened, just one of those things, okay?"

He pulled himself up from the floor. The bandages, which he had forgotten during their lovemaking, now felt like steel bands against his skin.

"But I don't know how something like that...."

She seemed genuinely baffled. In turn, he worked at being indifferent. Hey, he was a cowboy, and cowboys took a randy romp now and then and climbed back on their ponies. At the end of anything—a day, a fight, a love affair—a cowboy always gallops off into the sunset. No matter if there was a hole in your hat or your heart, you got the hell back up on that horse and took off. That's the way the script was written. "It's no big deal. Forget it. I will." Good show. He'd said his lines well.

She looked up, her eyes swirling with worry. "I thought...

It seemed that you... you felt something that—"

"What?" He laughed. He heard it as a brittle sound, as if something fragile had broken in midair. "Hey, don't sweat it. If you mean my mouth going all sentimental, that was just . . . just fancy words."

"Yes," she said uncertainly. "That's kind of what I meant."

Well, don't worry about it. "He looked down to where she sat, still huddled with her legs around her knees. She looked small and delicate. He could crush her—with his love, with his anger. Somehow, as he stared at her, the two feelings were one and the same. "I'm going to take a shower," he said. He stretched. His back hurt and his shoulder was sore again. Funny, how making love could make a man forget ninety-nine percent of the rest of his anatomy, to the exclusion of that one vortex of pleasure.

Once inside the bathroom, he reopened the door. Cassandra was buttoning her blouse. He began to speak, clearing his throat when his voice came out in a rasp. "Just out of, uh, curiosity . . ."

Cassandra's eyes were wide blue pools of sorrow and apprehension. God help him. He was losing himself to her, sinking into her soul.

"Yes . . . ?" she prompted listlessly. She didn't want to hear what he had to say. She was right of course. Some things were best left alone.

"Nothing. Forget it." He backed into safety, shutting the door securely behind him.

Leaning with his shoulder against the wood, he stared into the small square mirror above the sink. The face might have been a stranger's. There was a new look to him now; gone was the smirk of the rodeo-circuit star. The shadow of a boy's sorrow melded with a grown man's disappointment in life was lodged behind the outer screen he showed the world.

He thought of the men who wanted to kill him. If he died, it would not be so bad. Not so bad as feeling this way.

But he couldn't die. If not for himself, then for Charlie and Gordo, he must stay alive. Inside, filling him to the depths of his soul, was a need to make good on the dreams of the two other dumb unfortunates who believed in stories that ended happily ever after. He would have to survive.

Inside the bedroom, Cassandra listened for the sound of the shower. When the rush of water filled the stillness and she knew she could not be heard, she sat on the edge of the bed and sobbed.

She had never wanted this to happen! It was stupid and unexplainable and not in the best interests of anyone, certainly not her own. But the thing of it was, the terrible, awful thing of it was, she had never experienced such emotion in her life as she had with Alex Montana. Whatever had occurred in the cabin, it was nothing compared to what they had experienced in this room. They had made *love.*

What they had shared this morning could never come again in a lifetime.

It could never come again with any other man.

And that man could absolutely ruin what was left of her life. It was to have been such a nice life. There was to have been a prince. And now...

Cassandra covered her face and sobbed.

Chapter Nine

Alex insisted on driving when they left the motel. For a while, every time it was necessary to make a sharp turn, he winced with pain. Then, observing more closely, Cassandra came to the conclusion that he really didn't have to turn the wheel that sharply, and that in some strange way he was enjoying his physical agony.

She abandoned him as an object of her sympathy. Instead, she thought of Ralph and the cats, who deserved her concern far more. She would buy Ralph a new little mirror to make up for the neglect, and the cats would get a couple of squealing rubber mice, not to mention something especially delicious to eat.

Alex found the interstate leading to California, and they left the secondary route that wound through small desert towns. A few miles after they had crossed the border he took a detour at a junction displaying a sign for Fine Eats at Mamie Mahoney's.

"I'm really not all that hungry," Cassandra said as he shut the engine off in the parking lot.

"I am," he replied, and got out of the car.

He opened her side, and short of starting yet another war of wills, she had no other choice but to join him.

Inside, they were shown to a booth. He asked her what she wanted. "Coffee," she said. Her stomach was as confused as her mind. And every time she looked at Alex, something ached in her heart.

To the waitress he said, "She'll have the breakfast special." He scanned the menu. "Make that two breakfast specials, both scrambled. And coffees."

"I'm not hungry," she said sharply.

"Tough," he said just as angrily. "I don't want you dying on me."

"I hardly think I'm going to fade away in a morning's drive."

"The trouble with you is you hardly think at all."

"Oh, really?"

"You don't know anything."

She drummed her fingers lightly on the table, wondering if this was one of the times when it was wise to speak up or best to let the other guy ramble along on his own emotional trip. There were parallels to the problem in her martial arts training. The best course was always to use the attacker's energy against himself. In this case, she decided to compromise by neutralizing the situation. "Are you trying to start up again? Can't we just finish this drive in peace?"

"You have no idea which end is up or what's for your own good, or—what the hell's the use?" Suddenly he pushed himself out of the booth and went striding across the room. Cassandra watched until he disappeared into a hall marked with an arrow and the sign, Rest Rooms.

Fine, she thought, go soak your head. She chalked up the trip to the john as a minor victory. Still, his cutting remarks continued to echo in her head.

When he came back, their food had been delivered. Silently, across from each other, they both began to pick at the eggs. Neither of them lifted a fork to their mouths.

Alex put his fork down with too much force. It made a clinking sound on the edge of the plate. "So, look...I apologize. About before."

It took an effort to meet his eyes, but she managed. She was hurt, angry and very much confused. "So maybe I'm not a major brain trust. Maybe I've made a few dumb moves in my day. We all do. But I do the best I can."

"Maybe." He looked away. Then, returning his attention to her, said, "Or maybe you don't."

"What's that supposed to mean?"

He seemed about to tell her. Then his eyes flickered with indecision and he said, "Nothing." He busied himself with opening a small plastic container of grape jelly.

"No, you meant something, and I want to know what it was."

"Let's just finish this trip in peace," he said, throwing her statement back in her face.

Good show, Cassandra thought. A few lessons from Og the Absent One, and he'd be a credit to a long lineage of warriors. A rule of thumb—there were many rules of thumb connected to the philosophy propounded by Og— was to leave all negativity behind. Except sometimes. When was the "sometimes" relevant? That depended. And that was the problem with Og's particular philosophy. It was never entirely clear. She had asked him once why that was. And Og had replied in his bright, chirpy way, "Because my philosophy mirrors life, which is also not clear, in case you haven't noticed. The secret is to go

with life, not against it. Then all is revealed." She then had
asked how she could know the difference between when
she was going with life or against it. Og had said, "You
must feel it. After all, your life is up to you." Somehow not
too much of what Og had said then had made much sense.
But strangely, later, a great deal of his brand of mysticism
had come together as actual wisdom.

In the present situation, she had to determine if she
wanted to pursue the trail of negative vibrations related to
the topic at hand. Maybe this was one of the times when
Life was trying to teach her something. On the other hand,
this might be one of the times Life was merely trying to
hurt her feelings.

Alex was arranging the jelly on his toast with a knife.
She took the knife as a symbol that she must go forth into
battle. What the hell.

"Alex, I think we should talk about what you just
meant," she began calmly. Being centered in a state of inner peace was a major character component of the im-
peccable warrior. Actually, she was not one iota centered;
she was ticked off, and thus merely faking the peace and
tranquillity requirement. But, as Og always said, "If you
can't make it, fake it."

"I think a discussion would be a mistake," Alex replied. "Really I do."

"Yes, but you see, sometimes things are said to us that
we may not like to hear, but they are lessons that come our
way to help us grow." She manufactured a properly serene smile. "So, why don't you just spit it out, Alex?"

He returned a slightly evil smile. "Right."

Cassandra nodded for him to begin. Alex took an enormous, leisurely bite from his toast, then crunched for a
minute before commencing. "Well, Cassandra, you seem
to have a history of getting yourself involved in situations

and then begging out of them when things don't go the way you like, as if you had nothing to do with what happens. Around home we used to call that being a flake.''

"You mean with Og's business?''

"And that.'' They eyed each other stonily.

She was beginning to think this was one of the times Life was out to get her. But it was too late to back out now; she was already, as they say, going with the flow. Or perhaps just adrift. "And . . . and you mean about what happened with you and me . . . back there?''

"Now that you mention it. What the hell *was* that?'' he demanded. "God help me,'' Alex said quickly, looking at the ceiling, "I just broke my cowboy vow never to return to the site of a gunfight to count bodies.''

"I don't know what it was.'' This time it was she who looked away. "I really don't.''

"Well, then, what do you *think* it was?''

"Sex?''

"Try again.''

"Look,'' Cassandra said, "I don't even know you. You don't know me. We met three days ago. Before that we were strangers.''

"Now what are we?'' he demanded.

She kept her voice low, but the intensity of her feelings underlined each word. "We're nothing! Ships passing through the night, a one-night stand, a strange encounter of the first kind—call it anything you want!''

"You see. You're upset. I told you to forget the whole thing.'' Alex took a hard bite of his toast.

"No, you see.'' She waved her fork at him. "You see, Alex Rocky Montana. I'm going to get my car from your place, get in it and drive back to Los Angeles. You're going to go your way, and I'm going to go my way.''

"That's the beginning, the middle and the end of it?''

"Right." She put her fork down with a smack.

His fist came down on the table with a bang. "Wrong."

Cassandra jumped, along with several other patrons seated nearby. "You're making a spectacle," she said softly, lifting her coffee cup to her lips and trying to signal to the people around them that everything was A-okay in the booth with the two rumpled, crumpled souls glaring at each other, pounding tables and baring their fangs. Her hand trembled, and the coffee sloshed dangerously close to the cup's edge.

"Do you ever honor anything in your life?" he asked, deliberately speaking in a register audible to anyone who might care to listen.

Cassandra shifted uncomfortably in her seat. It was blackmail. He wasn't going to allow her to tune him out, change the subject, do anything to avoid the topic at hand. If she did, he'd just increase his volume and humiliate her. She didn't have to see the curious eyes watching them; she could feel them running over her body like ants.

Looking at her plate, which she could barely see through her rage and humiliation, she said in a register that was all but inaudible, "I wish you would lower your voice. Please. I would really appreciate that. If you would like to say something and have me respond to it, I promise to do my best. Okay? But, just don't...don't keep this craziness up, Alex, because for three days now I've had nothing but craziness. And Alex—" Cassandra looked up, her eyes dry, but barely "—I just don't think I have it in me to go through much more." Then one tear did fall.

The expression on Alex's face changed from righteous, furious indignation to alarm. No, it was more than alarm, Cassandra recognized as she quickly averted her face and surreptitiously brushed her napkin across her tears while pretending to pat her mouth. Alex looked downright compassionate. Kindness of any kind was always enough to do her in. An all-out war, she could handle, but kindness, that was another thing; she turned to mush.

"Cassandra," he said, and this time his voice was soft. "You are not the only one who's on a tightrope about to snap in two."

Cassandra closed her eyes rather than meet the truth of the preceding statement mirrored in his face.

"Look at me, please..."

Intense gray eyes enveloped her, the golden flecks exclamation points of feeling. Why did he have to be so beautiful? "I'm sorry about your situation." She took in a deep, guilty breath. "Truly. I don't know what more I can say or do to change anything, though."

"I do." He was quiet; he just stared at her, his eyes holding the meaning behind the two simple words he had just spoken.

"No. I told you how I felt about getting involved with killers. They're real killers, Alex."

"You're kidding, Cassandra. And all along I thought they were just a bunch of guys joking around."

"Go back home and get that gun, Alex. The one those guys left. Wear it. Use it, if you have to."

"I don't like guns," he said emphatically. "My thing is to stay alive, not to take the lives of others. I'm a firm believer of what goes around, comes around."

"So was Og," Cassandra said. "But he seems to have changed his tune. And his residence. And speaking of tunes, I never planned on having 'Taps' as my theme song."

"Lots of things happen that we don't plan on. In fact, you might have noticed that everything in life happens anyway. You get run over by a truck. You meet someone and you fall in love. You never plan on it."

"That's not true. Things don't just happen, not if you don't want them to. That is, they may begin to happen—I'll grant you that. But life doesn't necessarily have to railroad you clear down the track, either. I mean, you can say you want off the train before it goes too far." She was quiet for a moment, staring out the window by the booth. "Maybe you can't plan everything, but you can plan against some things. I planned on never falling in love with a married man. It might have happened—it's not like I haven't run across a suitor or two with a gold band on his finger. But it's possible to say no to the first drink after work. And then it's over, finished before it can begin and before anyone spills any tears." She turned from the window and faced him again. "Alex, I don't want to be involved with a marked man. I don't want things to get so out of control that I lose myself totally and completely, then one day I find out you're gone and I'm alone on this planet."

"Then keep me alive," he said simply.

"Keep you alive, keep you alive..." She shook her head. "Don't you understand? I've said it before. What do I have to do for you to hear me? I've told you I'm out of my league here. Maybe not so much in an actual physical sense, but emotionally. I'm not equipped to deal with honest-to-God murderers. Alex, any way you cut it, we've got too much against us."

"Okay," he said. "So I've said my piece. You've said yours. I think it went a little beyond the first drink you mentioned you'd turn down, but, uh, I think you're right."

"No, you don't."

"No, I don't. But maybe I will someday." He grinned his crooked smile. "If I live that long."

But for the radio, the remainder of the journey back to Alex's shack near Palm Springs was made in silence. Alex played a cowboy station. Cassandra figured he did it just to annoy her. All the songs were laments. Everyone had done someone else wrong. She half expected a dedication to come through: to Cassandra from Alex... thanks for ruining my life... not to mention ending it.

Cassandra closed her eyes and tried to block out the words of love gone sour, along with the sadness that kept creeping up on her whenever she thought of having to say goodbye to the man who still sat beside her. Every so often, he would reach forward and adjust the radio to another country and western station, or increase the volume, or decrease the volume. At those times his arm was close enough to touch, and she had to fight back the desire to hold him.

It was a long drive, but it seemed to have ended far too quickly when Cassandra glanced out the window, recognizing the mountain with the likeness of the vulture perched on its summit.

It was almost over—the ride and the relationship.

Only the relief she had hoped for didn't materialize.

Freedom would be hers again.

There was no alleviation of guilt.

Desperately she sought new arguments in favor of severing the relationship. She was only one person, and she could only handle so much responsibility. For one thing, there were the financial problems to face when she got back to Santa Monica. That crisis was enough to occupy any one person completely for a good long while. But finances seemed to have dimmed in significance beside the issue of her personal feelings for a man who was—she sternly reminded herself—not even remotely a contender for the role of Prince Charming.

Alex made a turn into the property on which the shack was located. Cassandra stared out the side window. She was careful to keep her face averted at an angle where she couldn't see Alex. She had to be strong now. In the last moment she didn't want to weaken in her resolve to end their personal and professional relationship then and there.

Alex sniffed. "Smell something?" he asked abruptly.

Her first thought was the engine, but then the unmistakable odor of a real fire caught her sense of smell. "A fire somewhere."

Alex's mouth drew into a tight line. "There isn't a somewhere. There aren't any trees. There isn't anything. There's only my place."

They looked at each other.

"I don't see any smoke," Cassandra said, searching the sky for evidence that she was right.

"There's a mountain over there," Alex returned. "It blocks a lot of space."

The plaintive cowboy songs had turned to annoying static; the reception was cut off by the mountains that partially surrounded the area. It couldn't have been late, but already shadows were forming on the ground as the sun shifted position and dipped behind some of the higher peaks.

The car had to make a sharp turn before clearing one of the canyons. Then, in the stretch before them, they had a clear view of Alex's cabin.

It was still smoldering, but much of it remained.

Off to the side, Cassandra's Fiat had been turned over, and it looked like a large green disabled bug.

There was nothing either of them could say, the vision before them said everything on its own.

Alex had already slowed the car. Now he brought it to a standstill. The engine gurgled as they stared straight ahead.

Suddenly Alex's attention shifted slightly. His eyes squinted as he leaned forward in his seat and twisted to catch a difficult view off to the side.

"What?" Cassandra asked, unable to make out what interested him.

Alex slumped back against the seat. "Nothing."

"No. It was something."

"I thought I saw something move."

"Someone?" Her voice was apprehensive.

"Something," he repeated, but not with conviction. "It might have been a coyote or a mountain lion. Maybe a big bird."

"Or them..."

Alex looked straight at her. "Cassandra, I hate to tell you this, but whether or not you like it, it's just possible this is one little drama you aren't going to be able to bow out of before the final curtain."

She felt the blood leave her face. Her skin turned cold, as if ice water spread slowly over her.

"I have nothing to do with your engine," she said.

"You know that, and I know that, but do they know that?"

"Why should they think otherwise?"

Alex shrugged. "Who knows how people like that think. Maybe they're just plain mean to the core. Or maybe they've got some great master plan worked out to destroy me and you've become part of it."

"I don't know why you're saying that."

"Because that's the way it is."

"You're just saying it to frighten me, Alex. You're trying to get me to stay on the job. But it's Og's job. His turf is the rough stuff, and I'm out, out, out."

Alex nodded, saying nothing more. Then he started the car forward again, rolling slowly toward the cabin. His eyes were scanning the entire area. "Okay," he said, inching along in the vehicle. He nodded ahead. "See that can?"

Cassandra looked to where she thought he meant. Beside her car was a large metal gas container.

"They were going to set fire to the Fiat, but didn't," she said, puzzling over the situation aloud.

"No, they didn't. Now why would that be?"

"Because..." She thought about it. "They heard us coming and—"

"Nope. They would have had to take the same way out. They've been long gone, babe. It was someone else," Alex said thoughtfully. "Someone else must have showed up here, and the bad dudes took off. Whoever it was probably stopped the fire."

"Who?"

"You tell me."

They parked in front of the shack. Alex went gingerly up the charred steps. He had some papers stashed inside: lists of parts for the engine, cost estimates, test results; nothing, he said, that he couldn't survive without, but nevertheless better to have than not to have. Cassandra waited outside, watching him feel his way into the shack. Some of the boards gave out, and he had to leap quickly to solid footing as they crumbled beneath him.

The smell of burned wood and smoldering mattress was noxious, and while Alex rummaged around inside, Cassandra drifted farther from the house where the fumes weren't as potent.

She was examining the damage to her car when a glint of something bright bounced off her windshield. Starting, her nerves already on edge, she responded at once, looking up and darting for cover at the same time.

But there was nothing to see but the serene landscape of desert floor and the steep face of mountains rising from the valley. A blackbird flew out of a craggy rock formation halfway up the nearest mountain. It cried out, irate at something, and flew overhead, flapping wildly. Then, simultaneous to the complaint, a small gravel and boulder landslide began in the same area the bird had left.

Cassandra watched, straining her eyes and ears to make out the cause of all the activity.

"Alex," she called. "Alex!"

Alex appeared in the door, alarm on his face.

"Look!" She pointed in the direction of the tumbling scenery. "A bird just flew out, and now everything's started to come down." Almost as she spoke, the miniature avalanche ceased its downward flow.

Alex shook his head. "Could be anything from a man to a lizard marauding a nest." He squinted into the distance. "Your basic kind of man couldn't make it up there. And if he could, why would he want to? Whoever was here is long gone. They came and got what they wanted, did what they wanted, and I guess they figure they'll catch up with me later. You're just spooked."

"The papers are gone?"

"Of course. Come on," he said, inching his way carefully across the porch and jumping to the ground rather than risk tripping over what remained of the stairs. "I'm taking you back to Los Angeles. I don't think you're going to be driving that home today." He looked toward the Fiat.

Cassandra shook her head, wondering what she was going to do without wheels. "They kind of worked it over. It's completely dented on one door, and they pulled off the rear bumper. Wasn't enough they had to put it on its head. It's like they had some kind of temper tantrum or something."

"Yeah, well, who likes to have their plans spoiled?"

Chapter Ten

To reenter Los Angeles was to enter another world. The desert and all that had occurred within it over the past two days seemed to belong to another realm entirely. The only thing that made Cassandra feel that any of it had been real was the presence of Alex beside her and the continuously friendly gurgle of the engine; the engine, Cassandra reminded herself, that was at the crux of all this misery.

It was going on four in the afternoon before Alex pulled up before her Santa Monica address. The night was already settling in, and an evening mist was rolling up from the ocean. Minute drops of moisture appeared on the car's windshield, making Cassandra wish for an honest-to-goodness rainstorm; something definite and tumultuous rather than this creeping, nothing, namby-pamby weather. Something definitive, that's what she wanted. Thunderclaps and deluges would be nice. Lately her life had come to seem like a way station. She wanted big physical boundaries and forward movement that swept her along with it—not this . . . this . . . purgatory of existence.

"This one?" Alex asked, checking out her neighbor's house.

"Uh-uh, that one," Cassandra corrected. "The one with the sad-looking cats." Both Hunka and Munka sat crouched on the porch. With the waxy green tendrils of ivy looping down in intricate tangles, the cats resembled two furry miniature sphinxes at the mouth of a cave.

"Hostile-looking creatures," Alex commented.

"Hungry," Cassandra defended. "They're too hungry for hostility. When they're really mad, it's much worse," she said, peering at them through the window . . .

It was quiet for a moment. The time of reckoning was finally upon them.

"Well . . ." she began.

"Well . . ." he followed, their two voices overlapping in accidental harmony.

They laughed then, again at the same time, both obviously embarrassed and nervous.

"Thanks for the lift home," she said.

"It was the least . . ."

"Sure was," she said. Her hand moved to the door handle.

"I'll, uh, see what I can do about the Fiat. I'll turn it right side up and see if it can be glued together again. You ought to be able to limp along in it for a few thousand more miles."

"Maybe I'll just call my insurance agency and have them give it a decent burial." She hesitated. "No, maybe I'd better not. They'll just raise my rates on anything new I get. Besides, they'll probably think I trashed it. Who would bother with such a clunker? Not even the thieves around this neighborhood ever touched it. Beneath their dignity, I guess.''

"It seemed to have a certain charm,'' he interjected chivalrously.

Cassandra hated him when he was so nice. It seemed like a plot against her. And to make matters worse he was looking at her sadly, and she couldn't bring herself to look away. She wanted to, but she couldn't. In a drifting voice, unconnected to her being, she said, "A lot of personality anyway.''

It was quiet again, and then suddenly Alex bolted from his side and was clear around the car and opening her door before she could protest the necessity of the polite gesture.

Stepping out, she was careful to avoid eye contact. She looked beyond his shoulder. "So, uh, it's been real…'' Her eyes darted to his face, then quickly away. If she could have run the entire way to the house, she would have, but instead she began to back off like a normal person saying goodbye. Each second seemed to last an hour; every step was a mile taken with a thousand-pound weight on her heart. Her entire being was afflicted: a lump in her throat, eyes stinging, rubber ankles, all the terrible symptoms of attachment to another human being. She cast her eyes heavenward. When the hell was it going to rain? Let it be now, she thought. Let it flood. Let the rains come and wash me downstream, out of my miserable existence.

She continued the retreat. But Alex advanced.

"I'll see you to the door,'' he explained, responding to what must have been the questioning, or possibly fearful, look in her eyes.

"You don't need to do that.''

"It's part of my upbringing. I always see women to their doors. My mother taught me that. My father taught me to try to get in the door." He grinned. "A joke," he said.

"Sure."

They walked together up the stone path leading to the immobile, glowering fur balls stationed on the porch.

"Hi, guys," Cassandra said, stooping to stroke the two cats, who remained frozen in their dignified poses.

"Affectionate devils," Alex commented wryly. "I can understand why you wanted to rush home to them. Do they ever move? Maybe blink?"

Cassandra let the slight go. Most times she would have defended Hunka and Munka, who really did have rather unique personalities when they weren't sulking. But her attention had moved to her mailbox, which was stuffed to overflowing with mostly To Occupant mailers, and—as she soon discovered—an ominous, official-looking letter from a bank.

The other mail fluttered to the ground as she fumbled to peek into a torn corner of the crisp white envelope bearing her name. Alex collected the dropped pieces and began to hand them back to her. Then he saw her face. "Hey...hey, what's wrong?"

She had pulled the letter out from the envelope and was now merely staring at its contents, her eyes frozen.

"Look, you can just call me Alex the Psychic Wonder, but, uh, I get the impression Rome just fell."

"What?" Cassandra looked up.

"I said, something terrible has just happened in your life. And you're about to deny it."

"It's nothing."

"Nothing. Fine. And will you accept that I'm Abraham Lincoln?"

She fumbled around in her purse for her keys. This time when she lifted her head, she wasn't able to hide her feelings. A tear fell onto the leather bag.

"Hey!" Alex took her chin in his hand and forced her to look at him. "What's going on?"

Cassandra bit her lip, tried to avert her face from his intent scrutiny. "Balloons... it's about balloons," she said.

"Balloons?"

"Yes, balloons." Turning, she unlocked the door and was about to stumble in when Alex pulled her back, saying, "Tell me."

The cats also moved forward expectantly, and the three—Alex, Hunka and Munka—waited for the explanation.

"My house—" Cassandra said, her voice wavering. "My house is going into foreclosure if I don't make my balloon payment."

"Oh." Alex remained motionless, his face registering understanding of the crisis.

She shook her head, half sadly, half with disbelief that such a thing could be true. "When I took out the loan, you know, I never thought—"

"We never do," Alex said. "We don't think about—"

"Disasters really happening."

"And when they do—"

"It's hard to believe."

"I wish there was something I could do," Alex said. "Honestly. If I could help..."

"Yeah," Cassandra said, recognizing her own words in a similar situation. "Thanks, anyway. For caring." She turned again and started to move inside with the mail and the cats.

"No problem," Alex said, still watching her. He waited a moment, then turned and moved slowly down the steps.

Cassandra was closing the door, partly peering through the lessening crack at him—it would be her last look—when Alex bounded back up the steps and said, "Wait a minute...dinner! How about tomorrow?"

Cassandra held the door where it was. With one eye, she peeked out at him. "I don't think so, Alex."

"Why?"

"It's just not in either of our best interests."

"Eating has always been high on the interest list of all human beings."

"Alex, in case you haven't noticed, we aren't like most human beings. We're being hunted and tormented by crazed maniacs. I'd like to extricate myself from the entire situation. I have balloons to worry about. Dying is just out of the question at the moment. I realize you have your own priorities in life, but for me, dying will just have to wait."

"Well, that's fine. So we won't die," he said cheerfully. "We'll simply dine. Tomorrow at seven. I'll be by to get you. It'll be a great evening—you'll see. Totally normal. Wine, candles, maybe some Italian food, real waiters, no bullets through the window or poison in the sauce..."

"Alex..."

"Look, Cassandra, everyone's got to eat. Even us. And this is going to be a free meal for you. Don't be dumb—just go with the invitation."

"Okay." But it was reluctant.

"Not a hell of a lot of enthusiasm, but okay, I'll go with it anyway. Give me your number. I'll call you later when I find a hotel and give you mine. Just in case."

"In case?" Cassandra said apprehensively, opening the door wider.

"In case you might like to, uh, talk." He smiled and winked lasciviously.

Cassandra gave him a corresponding dirty look, then tore off a check stub with her printed address and telephone number and handed it to him.

"Good," he said, examining the information. "I'll try to get someplace close by."

"Why?"

"Well, like I said, in case you'd like to—"

Obviously the previous look hadn't withered him as intended. "I wouldn't," she said. "I wouldn't." She closed the door.

On the other side she heard him call. "Hey! You never know for sure!"

Inside, the house was very quiet. For a moment she stood just inside the tiny foyer opening to the living room, getting the feel of her own private, secure space again. She waited for all the good feelings she usually experienced upon entering her house to come rushing forth, but they didn't. Something was missing from the atmosphere. She couldn't place what it was, but she felt it.

There were no lights on, and she thought that perhaps if she turned on a lamp or two, she could get the old inner glow back as well. With the cats padding anxiously beside her, she moved first about the living room and then into the kitchen, switching on lights.

"I'll feed you in a minute!" she said to the whining animals. "A minute. Okay, okay...now." It was too easy to intimidate her, she thought to herself as she took out a can of cat food and ran it through the electric opener. Even the cats could tell her what to do and when. And Og sure did. That Og. And now...now look what she had gone and done. She had allowed Alex to coerce her into another meeting. Dinner tomorrow. Well, she would tell him no when he called tonight. It would be much easier on the phone. Things were always more difficult when you stood nose to nose. Especially when a nose belonged to such an appealing face. Alex wasn't exactly conceited, but she knew he had a pretty good grip on how far his charms could take him. And with her, they had taken him way too far.

Cassandra issued a sigh, encompassing all her past weaknesses.

"Here, you poor babies," she said, and placed the two small dishes of food on the floor, checked the cats' water and watched for a few seconds as they began to devour their repast. "When I go to the market, I'll get something wonderful for you. Fresh salmon. With hollandaise. Promise."

Hunka and Munka were abandoned for a long bath. It was a favorite ritual, a reward for withstanding the pressures of the day. The bathroom was old and big. Tile squares covered all the walls, the counter holding the sink, and even the floor, with the predominant color being a pale green interspersed with triangular tiles of shiny black and white. It was really quite an ugly color combination. The green was sickly and nondescript, doing nothing for anyone. But, like many homely people, whose very deficiencies were worked around to serve in their best interests, the room took on a certain individualistic élan.

Early into her occupancy of the house, Cassandra had found a good deal on an old freestanding claw foot tub. Hiring a handyman, she had helped him rip out the old built-in bath and installed the romantic relic in its place. It was white enamel and chipped in a couple of places, but it made a statement on behalf of survival. Survival was something with which Cassandra could definitely identify, and never more so than on this particular night.

While the water filled the tub, she lit the candles. They were placed on the counter, on a plastic stool, on top of the toilet tank and on two hanging shelves. In all there were ten pink tapers positioned in pink ceramic holders, loosely resembling unfolding roses. She had picked them up at a high school ceramic sale. It was only a beginning class, and the girl had said she was still working on petals. She thought she'd have them down by next year, if Cassandra wanted to come back.

When she finally eased herself into the steaming water, Cassandra was beginning to feel at home again. The initial sense of the house being less complete than when she had left it three days before had dissipated somewhat in the waves of steam rising from the water and in the companionable shadows dancing against the tile.

Whatever peace she found was short-lived, however. Whereas in the past she might have built castles out of the vapor drifting off her kneecaps, tonight she saw faces—no, a face, a particular face; a particular face of a particular man. Sloshing about to distract her mind didn't help any. It only called attention to her desperate state of mind, which had to resort to acrobatics rather than being able to relax into a good soak. Alex Montana haunted her, even in this most hallowed space—the shrine of candlelight and soap bubbles.

Her only hope would come with time and distance. There must be a lot of both put between them. Accordingly she began to practice what she would say when Alex called. Several speeches were begun and discarded, and the best was tested through a dry run presented to Hunka, who had slunk into the room, his humor much improved after eating. She wished Alex was there to see Hunka now, moving about like a regular cat.

"...and so, Alex...it's in our mutual best interests to agree, here and now, to sever all communication for all time..."

It sounded like a state address. Even Hunka yawned.

"Okay, so it's a little stiff. Give me a break," she be-seeched her unimpressed audience. She thought for a mo-ment. "How about this one? We're doing truth here, all the way, taking it to the limit, riding it to the max..." She looked directly into Hunka's yellow eyes. They blinked.

She began. "I like your body. I would like to make love with you every day and every night. But this is a danger-ous proposition because, as I've said before, one or both of us could get blown to smithereens. And there's some-thing else. You are not a prince. You are of the frog vari-ety. And no matter how much I enjoy sleeping with you and looking into your eyes when we speak, and laughing at your sometimes funny but often stupid jokes, I happen to know what befalls a girl who lowers her standards for those particularly superficial but admittedly compelling reasons."

Very encouraging... Hunka was listening.

"That was it," she said. "So... how'd it play?"

Hunka arched his back, stretched and meandered out of the room. Cats were harsh critics.

She had been out of the bath for two hours when the telephone rang. At its sound, her heart gave a happy little leap, and she found herself rushing to stop the ring.

"Hello?" she said. Silence on the other end. Then a click. More disappointed than she liked to admit, she re-placed the receiver. Maybe it was a bad connection. Maybe it was a wrong number. Maybe it was Alex, who had de-cided upon hearing her voice that they should, as she had insisted so strenuously, end the relationship after all. Such things were possible, sudden changes of mind.

For the next hour she moved restlessly about the house in her pink silk robe, watering plants and compulsively dusting and plumping cushions. Now and again she would eye the telephone. On its little semi-antique telephone table, it sat as still and silent as Hunka and Munka who, from the sofa, watched her frenzied activity with the haughty disdain of aristocrats observing a peasant perform menial tasks.

The phone rang again.

Cassandra lunged for it, then waited for three full rings before actually picking it up.

Casually she said, "Hello..."

"Hi!"

Her heart smiled. A radiant warmth filled her. Over the phone, Alex sounded so real and solid and safe and happy and wonderful. "Alex...?" She feigned restraint.

"Yeah," he said, and she knew, in that one word, was an underlying question tinged with jealous insecurity: Who else did you think it could be? "Got a pen or something?"

"Ummm..." she said nonchalantly, and quickly grabbed a pencil and a piece of paper from the small drawer beneath the phone. Her speech wasn't polished enough yet. Maybe tomorrow.

"Ready?"

"Ummm." She wrote down the number and repeated it back.

"So, I'll see you tomorrow at seven," he said.

"Alex!" She couldn't believe it! He was going to hang up. There was to be no conversation. No pitch to come back over that night. No nothing. The abrupt disconnection threw her off.

"Yeah?"

"Uh, I just..." Her mind had become the proverbial blank slate. "Is it a nice room?"

"I don't think a president's ever slept here."

"Oh. Well."

"Cassandra? I don't mean to pry, but are you okay? You sound a little drifty, know what I mean?"

"I've been dusting," she said.

There was a pause. "Oh. That explains it. So, anyway, catch you tomorrow."

And then he was gone. Just like that he had hung up on her. No corny speech about counting the minutes until they met again, no annoying sexual innuendos, no inappropriate attempt to place his body at her disposal that night.

With nothing else to dust or plump, and no phone calls to wait for, she had only sleep to occupy her time. Before settling in, she dragged herself around the house, checking doors and windows, shutting off the lights. Hunka and Munka sauntered elegantly past her with their tails up while she was going down the hall to her bedroom. A moment later she heard the squeak of their cat door as they departed on some nightly social adventure.

Sleep was only an ideal dream not to be realized. Cassandra waited impatiently for her lids to grow heavy, and they did. But her mind spun in circles, and a yearning— partly emotional, partly physical—possessed her body. For years she had gone without serious male involvement in her life and had managed well enough. Certainly there had been lonely moments, moments like the present, when she had desired sex, but she had withstood the temptation to abandon her vision of her prince for the satisfaction of mere ordinary male companionship.

But tonight was unlike the other times when she had lain awake, lonely, needing a man's body. There was, she knew, something devastatingly urgent in this longing to experience a union with— Cassandra sat up. *Hell,* she thought. It was *him*, Alex, who had done all of this to her. He had set her up. He had set her on fire. He had set her off-balance. He had made her want him, just as if she were any other sex-starved lonely woman whittling her life away while waiting for the man of her dreams to come waltzing into her empty life. For all she knew he could be with someone else right at that moment.

She slipped her legs to the edge of the bed and considered this possibility. That's why he had taken so damned long to call her. He'd probably gone to get dinner and met someone.

She stood up, her eyes blurring as she watched the drama playing across her inner screen: Alex, right now, lying in bed with some little floozy.

Grabbing her robe from the bed, she drew it on, then took off for the kitchen in a fury. Swinging open the refrigerator door, she withdrew a bottle of milk, slammed the door shut, took a small pot from the bottom cupboard, then slammed the cupboard shut. It took a couple of minutes for the milk to warm, and when it had, she realized she had poured far too much. She was thinking of nothing but that damned deceitful cowboy who had nothing but sex on his mind.

That was why, she thought miserably as she poured the warm milk into a cup, he hadn't hustled her over the phone. He'd already made a good score. Tonight belonged to the floozy; tomorrow would be her turn!

She swilled down the heated milk, which didn't relax her as she had intended but merely warmed the vengeance in her veins to a fine boil.

At that moment Hunka appeared in the frame of the cat door.

"Hello," Cassandra snapped. "Want some milk?"

Hunka stared up at her, his expression strange. He held her eyes, it seemed, as if out of deliberate intention to communicate some message.

"Milk?" she repeated again. Hunka spoke perfectly good menu, and that he didn't offer some sort of reply by wave of tail, or rub of body against leg, or a simple whine to get on with it, was unusual.

Cassandra poured the extra milk in a saucer anyway and placed it on the floor. Hunka merely continued to stare. The yellow eyes were intent, would not blink. "What? Oh. You've been out eating God knows what kind of junk food in the Andersons' garbage, haven't you? And protein, something healthy, is just real blah now. So fine. Munka is a whole heap more discriminating anyway." But Munka wasn't around.

Cassandra unlocked the back door and stepped out-side. It was impossible to see anything in the dark, so she reached back in and switched on the floodlight.

The back garden was presented in otherworldly focus. The fog that had begun late that afternoon was still thin in some areas, but in other places it was almost too dense to see through. Trees and shrubs were rendered in clumpy indistinct outline form. The large tree nearest the house had lost its leaves, and its bare branches now loomed over her like a spiny, gnarled hand. A chill passed through Cassandra, the kind that wasn't attributable to the damp.

"Munka?" she called softly. "Munka...a treat..."

There was no sign of the cat. Cassandra called a few more times, then stepped down the back stoop to peer around the corner of the house where the driveway came up the side. The driveway ended at the small single-car garage with an attached storeroom. She had always meant to convert it into a studio of some sort when she had time for a hobby.

Her eyes traveled beyond the freestanding structure of the garage to the back fence. In the filtered light, the re-cently painted white board fence glowed eerily. Behind the fence was an alley. Countless times Cassandra had stood in the same place on other nights, calling. Within seconds the cats would come stealing over the fence in response to her voice.

"Munka?" She waited, slightly apprehensive, but not knowing why. Then a quick shadow moved off to the right of the fence, and Cassandra smiled. "There you—" Both smile and word died simultaneously.

Clearly she had seen movement, a form of some kind. But it wasn't Munka, and whatever it was had slithered out of view before she could make out its size or establish any other kind of meaningful identification.

Backing slowly toward the stoop, she searched for further signs of the intruder—animal or human, it was impossible to tell. Whatever it had been seemed both large and small, visible and invisible all at once. The unknown was always puzzling and frightening.

Another movement.

Cassandra stood firm, her body immediately assuming a relaxed stance, her mind slipping into another mode where fear had no place. Alert down to her last cell, she bent her knees slightly and found her center.

And then a rushing form slipped into view.

Munka. The cat came dashing forward, as if running for its life. Relief came just as swiftly to Cassandra. The blood in her body began its circulatory process once again. Her heart took up its beat.

Behind the streak of fur the white fence continued to glow. Just as Munka bounded past and up the steps to the kitchen, a faint sound issued from the alley, as if something heavy had dropped to the other side.

Then all was quiet.

Cassandra backed into the house. Her fingers were numb as she secured the door's lock.

Turning, she saw the two cats staring up at her, talking to her with their four yellow eyes. She didn't like the message.

Chapter Eleven

I knew you'd break down sooner or later, and see things my way," Alex said as Cassandra let him into the foyer. "So which way's the bedroom?" His hands went to the top button of his sport shirt. It was all in fun, but his voice didn't match the levity of his words, and suddenly he asked, "What's happened over here?"

Cassandra stood before him, the sash to the pink robe pulled tightly around her waist. It hadn't taken Alex longer than ten minutes to get to her house after she had called. Her heart was still pounding, but not out of fear this time. Instead, she felt dizzy and weak and filled with an inexplicable urge to rush into his arms and bury herself, body and soul, in his being. She needed him. She truly needed him, for comfort, for love, for sex, for everything.

Yet she backed away. "Nothing really. That is, nothing that I could be sure of. Maybe I'm just spooked, as you put it, about all the stuff that's happened over the past couple of days. I didn't want to be alone. I thought maybe you weren't doing anything. So I called." The previous vision of Alex romping with the floozy in his motel room, insinuated itself into her mind again. She watched him for signs that she was right or wrong. If there had been a floozy, would he have left the floozy to come to her rescue?

No answer. Alex gave away nothing. That, too, could be a sign. But she didn't know what kind. Anyone knew that men who indulged in floozies as a regular diet were clever enough to hide the fact. Or perhaps Alex was simply innocent. She would die before she would ask him, of course. But then again, that was the issue here, wasn't it? Death.

She turned and drifted from the foyer into the living room. Alex checked to make certain the front door was locked before following her.

"I went out in back to call Munka and I thought I saw something. It was only a shadow—fast moving. And then I heard something. Very faintly. A sound, like something dropping to the pavement behind the fence. There's an alley there," she explained.

"You mean *someone* may have been out there."

"Yes," she said, her voice small. "It's the someone aspect I'm mostly worried about."

"You called the police?"

"No. I thought of it, but they'll just come out and look around, and you know as well as I do, they'll never find anything. So they'll tell me to keep the doors and windows locked and to report any unusual sounds. That sort of advice. Whoever it is, Alex—if it is someone—is good. I swear to you, they were in my backyard and I didn't even see them. They appeared and disappeared in plain view."

"That's better than good. That's scary."

They stared at each other again, in the way they always did when there was no way to make words match the moment.

"I know you don't want to hear this," said Alex, "but I'm afraid you're involved too deeply already. There's no way out of my mess, Cassandra, except to tough it out with me. Together we may be able to outwit, or outrun, those goons."

Cassandra turned away and walked over to the fireplace. On either side of it were slightly warped built-in bookshelves filled with books and plants in various whimsical containers. She fiddled with the leaves of one of the plants.

Alex came up behind her. "Don't worry," he said, "this won't last forever. I know you don't want to be with me. It'll just be until the show." His hand touched her shoulder, and with one finger he brushed her neck softly. She might have been a little cat.

The tenderness reduced her resistance. "I want to be honest," she said. "I mean, maybe I don't have much time left." The joke fell flat. "So I may as well come clean with you."

Alex stopped stroking her and waited. "Yeah?"

"I did see something out there tonight. But I also wanted you to be here." She was glad she didn't have to face him. What she was doing was semihumiliating. But she felt it had to be said.

"You missed me?" There was genuine surprise.

"In a sense."

"In a sense."

"I wanted you." She was burning from the touch of his hand on her neck. The fever was partly from shame and partly because even that slightest connection between them set a current zipping through every erogenous zone in her body. Confession was supposed to make a person feel good. She didn't feel good. She felt stupid. Dumb. Like crawling under the leaf she was holding.

Behind her she heard what she took as a slight chuckle. "So, you're after my body, are you?"

"Certainly not your personality!" And she started away, wishing she had kept her mouth shut about her feelings.

Alex grabbed her arm and spun her around. "So! And I thought you were different. But, no, you're just like all the others. Can't keep your hands off me. Another hot-blooded wench on the prowl. Oh, well, I guess I'll put you out of your misery."

"You're impossible," she said, struggling to avoid his mouth, which was making a sweeping tour of her upper extremities.

"I'm in love," he said, outmaneuvering her.

"Look, you don't have to say that."

She was beginning to give into her body's response. Beyond, her eyes rested on an ivy plant, its tendrils crawling along the shelf. The plant was growing in a ceramic container in the form of a castle. Very symbolic. It had little turrets, and windows in the turrets, and a big door that her prince would knock on one day.

"Yes, I do," Alex said.

Her heart was beating faster, and her eyes were filling with tears. This was the way it was supposed to be with her prince, but this guy—Alex Rocky Montana—wasn't him.

"Why?" she asked. "Why must you?" His mouth moved over her lips. She thought she would pass out from the chills running up her spine.

"Because it's polite," Alex said.

Cassandra froze, then pulled away with enough force this time to actually break their embrace.

"Well, you don't have to be polite," she said.

"Yes, I do," he countered with just as much vigor.

"And why is that?"

"Why? I'll tell you why." Alex marched over to the bookshelves and pointed. "See this?" It was the castle. "And this?" It was a pair of china figures, a man and a woman entwined, both in medieval garb. "This is what you're all about. This is what you're looking for in life. Do you think I'm stupid? You don't want me, an ordinary guy who happens to have some extraordinary, and real, passions to share with you. So, I figure that the way to make you happy is to fit into your dreamworld. If that's the only way I can reach you."

Cassandra was so humiliated she didn't know what to say. The truth was the truth. And in this case it made her appear ridiculous and childish, even petty.

"Maybe you ought to go."

"Okay," he said. "It's your house. Your life. Your funeral." Turning, he started toward the foyer.

"No," she said, "don't. Please. I'd like you to stay. Really."

Alex looked over his shoulder. "You know," he said, "you haven't exactly got the market cornered on fantasies."

"No?" Cassandra said softly, uncertain if he was coming or going, and now wanting him very much to stay.

"I've had a few of my own over the years."

"I wouldn't mind hearing about them . . ."

He shook his head. "Uh-uh. Talk about a fantasy, you lose it. A cosmic law."

"What about mine?"

"Yeah, well, every fantasy has its time limit. At the right moment they dissolve or they become real."

"It looks like mine dissolved."

"Sure looks that way. I don't wear a suit of armor, babe. Just boots and jeans."

He was looking at her with a curious, half-amused, definitely sad gaze. "So we'll just be who we are to-night," Cassandra said.

"That isn't going to work," he said, and opened the door.

"Why?" she rushed, crossing quickly to him before he could leave.

"Because I'm still going to be that same guy tomorrow."

"Maybe I'll be different."

Alex grinned. "That's a hell of a vote of confidence. To think a roll in the hay can change a woman's life."

Cassandra felt her face grow hot. She had to be flushing as pink as her robe. If he only knew. A roll in the hay had already changed her life. "Maybe," she said, and looked past him to the hall leading to the bedroom. "You never know."

Alex smiled slowly. "So let's find out."

Her room was small and cosy. There was flowered paper on the wall, and a tiny dressing table had a flounced chintz skirt with the same delicate country-English pattern. The curtains were white nylon gauze. A walk-in closet held a built-in dresser, and there was one Queen Anne chair used to throw her clothes over when she was too tired or lazy to put things away properly. Besides these there was only the queen-size bed which was much too large for the room's scale.

Amid the room's feminine furnishings, Alex loomed like a giant. She saw that the bandages were gone now, and with his shirt removed his skin gleamed smooth in the light from the hall. Everything about his presence in her room, not to mention his place in her life, seemed incongruous.

Yet he was here, and as Cassandra walked to the side of the bed and removed her robe, she considered something Og had once said. Everything in life fit together exactly as it should, he had told her. It was only man's limited perspective that didn't see the perfection of life's pattern. It wasn't the mind, but the heart, that sees. Of course Og was a scoundrel of the first order, but sometimes he seemed to know things that bore heeding.

For this night, for this one night, at least, she would attempt to see with her heart.

Alex slipped into bed beside her. He propped himself on his elbow and smiled his slanted, impossibly irresistible smile. "The truth. Has any other man ever been in this bed?"

"No."

"I didn't think so," he said, and the smile faded to a look of seriousness. "Then I am special," he said, and traced a finger to where the sheet covered her breast.

"Yes," she whispered, burning at his touch.

"And this will be special," he said. Slowly he moved the sheet down. His eyes remained linked to hers, even as he brought his fingers trailing along the curve of one bare breast. Cassandra closed her eyes, shivering from his touch.

His mouth moved over her flesh, softly at first, and then with more pressure as his own passion grew.

Yet gentle, somehow always gentle. The thing that amazed Cassandra the most, that took her by surprise the first time she had made love with Alex, was his underlying gentleness, a kind of innate sensitivity to her feelings that went along with the more aggressive side of his male nature.

Periodically her mind would rise out of the whirlpool of physical sensation. She would look at him full on, amazed, seeing him lean and hard and human and fully male, lying beside her—obviously as lost as she was to the strangely complete union they found in each other.

She was not one to become carried away by ordinary passions, but this, with Alex, was extraordinary. She seemed to fly through the air with him, carried on the wings of sensation.

"Alex..." she said, and the name was not a name but a symphony of sound contained in one word.

His hands brought her into him, controlling her, guiding her into an entirely different mode of lovemaking. Then it was her turn. She rose over him, slipping naturally into her new role of seductress and temptress, finding herself an expert in an art she had only just discovered. It was as if she had held crayons in her hand before, drawing only the outline of life; and now she painted with watercolors, her body a nimble brush rendering magnificent feelings. The texture of the canvas rose three-dimensionally out of the power released in their passion.

Alex entered her, silk and steel uniting. They held still for a moment, unable to move from the exquisite feel of their bodies joined together.

Then, in a rush of urgency, the movement began, and Cassandra was swept into the rhythm of his heartbeat. His legs trembled, linked to hers. Against her breasts, his chest rose and fell. With each brush of their bodies, her heart expanded, opening like a flower with a million unfolding petals. Her soul was burning into his, and his into hers. At last his mouth turned into a silent cry of ecstasy, and shuddering, she arched into him, her body an unending spasm of love.

"Cassandra..." he said much later, still fevered as he lay beside her. "I think a fantasy just bit the dust."

She leaned over and looked into his face. She had never seen a man who was that beautiful before. So perfect was he, she could barely stand to gaze upon him. Tears came to her eyes, and she closed them tightly, trying to keep in the feeling, the moment, the love, forever. And it was then that she knew how right Og had been, for with her heart open, she still saw the beautiful face before her. It was a sight that blinded one's ordinary vision. Only a heart could take in such magnificence.

When she did look with ordinary vision again, Alex was asleep.

She rose softly from the bed and slipped into the bathroom. When she returned to her bedroom, she glanced out the window into the back garden. The fence was there, cool and white, a shimmering screen against which any sort of drama might be enacted. The shadows were very quiet, it seemed. The night was waiting, watching.

Cassandra slipped back into bed and snuggled against Alex's warmth. His breath rose and fell. His heart beat against hers. She was a part of him.

Alex . . . if I lose you now . . .

Chapter Twelve

In the daylight the world was quite different. And so were they, Cassandra discovered. At the kitchen counter she watched Alex from the corner of her eye for signs of what he might be thinking or feeling as she poured another cup of coffee for herself. He sat at the small round table, spooning down dry cereal, which was all she had available for breakfast.

They were both dressed and ready to make the most of what the day brought, she in a black sweatsuit, Alex in slacks and sport shirt with a navy pullover. He looked wonderful to Cassandra, not like a ramshackle ex-rodeo star, but maybe even like a corporate executive on the rise to boardroom heights. Maybe even—bite her tongue—somewhat like her prince, although that was probably going too far. It was light playing tricks on her.

For a change the morning wasn't clouded over. Something faintly resembling sunlight was drifting through the panes of glass over the sink. In the living room Ralph was chirping and trilling for all he was worth. Even from the kitchen he could be heard bounding about his cage, bashing his bell and crashing against the metal frame. Maybe the sun and the song were signs of life on the upswing.

Cassandra brought her cup back to the breakfast table where Alex sat. As she listened to him speak, he seemed less and less princelike and more and more his usual self. In the rhythm of mundane life, he spoke of the engine and of how poor Jerry Friedman had inadvertently helped to make a brilliant modification to the original design by comparing the pistons to the force of light emanating from the facets of a diamond.

Alex seemed downright exhilarated to share this tidbit of science with her. She wanted to be impressed but really couldn't grasp the concept, even after it was explained twice. It sounded "nice," she said. "Nice," was the best she could make out of it. Her only truly heartfelt comment was, "Poor Jerry Friedman."

Alex then became quiet for a time, and so did she.

"That was great," he said exuberantly when he had finished with breakfast.

"You can save the gentlemanly heroics. It was just dry cereal," Cassandra pointed out.

He stared down at the bowl as if the news had come as a revelation. Then, looking up at Cassandra, he said, "I'm going to head out to the desert and see if I can collect a few of my tools."

At his announcement her heart constricted. "Do you think you should go out there alone?"

"You want to come? It's a nice day. We could drive into Palm Springs and have lunch."

Of course they both knew perfectly well he wasn't just inviting her on a ride. It was the old issue again—was she or wasn't she involved with the enterprise of dealing with the goons? But before she had time to reply, Alex gave her a break and said, "No, better stay here. I may not have any room for you once I get all the stuff loaded up."

It was a lie, and they both knew it. Alex was buying them both time. What they had established in the moonlight through the flesh existed tenuously in the morning light. Neither of them wanted to lose that thin connection between heaven and earth. Not yet anyway.

So, in the end, Cassandra went along with the stalling of reality and waved goodbye to him from the driveway after saying that he could use the garage to store his things until he found a permanent place.

With Alex gone the house seemed to ring of emptiness. And yet, periodically, as she went about her routine of straightening up, she imagined the ring of his voice as it had sounded that morning when he had called to her from the shower, and the echo of his laughter when she had burned the toast, and...

Cassandra looked down at the bed she had been making and suddenly burst into tears. If she wanted to keep Alex, she had to give up everything else. No more dreams. She realized that her life had held a certain unrealized anticipation for a long while: she was much like a person who had ownership of a perpetual lottery ticket, promising great fortune. It made almost no difference anymore whether the number was called. The great thrill was the ongoing hope that holding the lottery ticket provided in her life. *Her life*. With a start, she remembered she actually had such a thing and that she had damn well better take care of it.

In contrast to the moonlight euphoria and her idealized dreams of the future, there existed, here and now, the absolutely real situation of how to save her house—not to mention that she would have to earn some immediate income to buy food. And there was Ralph. And Hunka and Munka. She had dependents.

One thing she had always hated was to look for jobs. She especially detested applying for civil service jobs, which was basically what teaching had become in a city the size of Los Angeles. It wasn't nearly so bad to look for more ordinary work, such as waitressing. There seemed to exist a general element of sympathy with restaurant owners and bar owners, as if both she and they belonged to some sort of lesser club in the world. But those kinds of jobs seemed to belong to a past she had long left, and the most logical alternative for employment was to resume teaching. But that required dealing with the Great Educational Bureaucracy, overseen by Oz-like personalities who never seemed to deal in specifics—handing out forms when you wanted a job and answering questions in obscurities unrelated to what was asked. One of life's great miracles was that anyone ever got hired before they died of old age or starvation.

Nevertheless, she would make the attempt to seek either permanent teaching employment or work as a substitute until they found a full-time slot she could fill.

Five hours later she returned home. The trip had proved futile. She had returned from the land over which Oz presided with no job, no hope for one, and not even a tin heart. Dorothy had done a whole lot better.

It seemed that in the relatively short while since she had left the profession new rules and regulations had been passed. If she would like to reenter the hallowed ranks of her peers, she must show proof of having completed twelve college units in specialized educational classes. The lady who had informed her of this had been colorless as still swamp water and had smacked her lips delightedly upon delivering the news. Cassandra would have liked to have smacked the woman. But she couldn't and didn't; after all, she was officially a lethal weapon. Anyway, some fine day, some other person would wreak revenge on the mole behind the counter. That had been Cassandra's sole consolation on the bus back to her house.

Once home, she covered Ralph's cage, shutting him up, then sank into a corner of her sofa and considered crying for twenty minutes or so. But nothing was left in her, not even tears. Instead, she merely stared at her hardwood floor, her eyes compulsively tracing around the edges of several small fake oriental carpets. From the floor, her eyes moved to the walls, from one print to the next, and then to each and every stick of furniture, so loved, so polished, so dusted, so temporary. Soon these things, along with the walls that contained them, would no longer be hers.

And then, with this certain realization of her impending fate, she did cry. Sobbing, she prayed for a miracle. If there was a God, then let some other unknown relative croak and leave her a bundle of money. She prayed that oil would gush from her backyard. She prayed that the prince she had been waiting for all these days would suddenly appear and make everything right again.

It was during this request that the doorbell rang.

Cassandra decided at first not to answer it. Her nose was red, her face was blotched and her eyes were puffed. But the person rang again and followed that demand by pounding against the wood. She then remembered Alex and peeked out the curtain to check if it might be him, returned early.

What she saw was a vision.

She closed the curtain, then reopened it, certain her eyes had deceived her.

No. It was still there.

Parked before her house was a long white stretch limousine. Standing by the driver's side was a uniformed driver, and at the front passenger's side, another man in an elegant suit.

The pounding continued, with short bursts from the bell.

It was a hell of a position to be in, she thought as she moved to the door: curiosity versus humiliation.

Swinging open the door, she stared into the face of a man dressed in a dark suit, white shirt and tasteful tie. Her first thought was that he was a kind of super Bible salesman. Her second thought was that this might be her prince. Her third thought was that the bank had come early to repossess her house.

"Yes?" she answered.

"You're Cassandra Burke?"

"Yes." She was having trouble concentrating. All she could think of was her red nose and how bad she looked.

"Alan Greely. I represent Philip Matthison."

"Philip Matthison?"

"As his assistant. You do know Mr. Matthison . . . ?"

Cassandra nodded slowly, trying to take the whole thing in and make sense of it. Everyone knew Philip Matthison. Matthison was one of the leading biggies in entertainment law, representing screen and nightclub idols in everything from their divorce cases to serious brushes with the police. Actually, Philip Matthison's own life was as colorful as some of his clients. Lots of nasty things had been written about him, but it was on record that he only laughed, saying that anyone who had power was bound to incur the wrath of those who did not. And Philip Matthison certainly had power. His influence ran all the way from the elite of the social and cultural sets to city hall, even extending as far away as Capitol Hill. Yes, Cassandra knew who Philip Matthison was.

She was mostly surprised that Philip Matthison knew who she was.

They went into the living room, and Alan Greely took a seat and proceeded to explain.

"From time to time, my employer—Mr. Matthison—has occasion to hire someone in the protection business to perform personal services for him. He, of course, has regular staff who look after this particular aspect of his personal life on a routine basis. But sometimes there are special instances when he seeks outside professional expertise. This is one such instance. To this end, I was instructed to contact Ogata Kenzo. He came highly recommended as perhaps the best practitioner of martial arts in the city—"

"In the country," Cassandra corrected.

"Yes," Alan Greely conceded. "Arguably the best in the world."

"Now that Bruce Lee is gone."

"Actually, our problem is that Ogata Kenzo is also gone."

"This is true," Cassandra said, experiencing the familiar pangs of humiliation by association yet again. "I'm afraid I can't help you locate him. I have no idea where he is, or when he may be returning."

"He sounds very mysterious."

"Og's ways *are* strange. And yet..." To go further would make her sound loony.

"You were saying?"

"Nothing."

"Please..." Alan Greely smiled slightly. He had gray eyes that seemed never to change expression.

"It's just that strange as Og is—or was—he always seems to tie things up in the end so that everything makes a crazy kind of sense."

"I see." Greely was silent for a moment. "You don't by any chance think that Ogata Kenzo may have met with some kind of permanent misfortune, do you?"

"Permanent, like death?"

"A consideration..."

Considerations she had, and by the spadeful. But she had never made this a consideration. It seemed, even now, inconceivable that Og would ever go the way of ordinary mortals like poor Jerry Friedman. She had thought of Og as living on and on, like some sort of super cat, with a thousand and one lives.

"No," she answered emphatically. "Og is somewhere, safe and sound."

"I see. You can be sure of that?"

Oddly Cassandra didn't get the impression that Alan Greely was pleased by her insistence that Og was alive and well. "As sure as I am that he's the best in the business."

"We understand you were his best student. And also his business partner."

"You know a lot," Cassandra said, wondering if she ought to feel pleased or worried that she had come under the scrutiny of such an illustrious personality as Philip Matthison. "How'd you find all of this out? How'd you even find me?" she asked. Her address and telephone number weren't listed in the public directory, and she had always kept her residence sacred and private from any dealings with the public.

Greely smiled but only with his lips, his gray eyes remaining reserved. "We have our ways," he said.

He had meant the phrase as a joke, as a parody of the old line in forties black-and-white war movies. Cassandra smiled—kind of. It didn't take a lot of brains to figure out the flip response was his way of telling her he was there to ask questions, not provide answers. Her dealings with sophisticates like Greely were limited to what she saw in movies. This was the real thing, and she already knew she was outclassed in psychological moves. If this were a chess game, the guy would certainly already be ten plays ahead of her in his mind.

While Cassandra was thinking, Greely looked about the room. "Very nice," he commented.

"Thank you." The words caught slightly in her throat. Sure the room was nice, but it wasn't going to be her room for long.

"We'd like to offer you the job we had intended for your associate, Ogata Kenzo." He waited, allowing her time to digest the statement.

"I'm not in Og's league," Cassandra explained truthfully.

"But you were his foremost disciple."

"Streams flow into oceans, too. But that doesn't make them oceans."

Greely stared at her, perhaps in annoyance that she was offering some resistance to what had already been carefully planned.

"I realize that," he said. "But you see, we feel that short of having your teacher working in our behalf, you're truly our best bet for the job we have in mind. We've considered this very carefully. Mr. Matthison himself has made this determination, and Mr. Matthison is a very thorough and extremely cautious business man." Greely paused. "The job will pay forty thousand dollars."

Cassandra stared. She owed thirty-five thousand on the balloon payment. She could pay off the loan, plus have five thousand left over to put in the bank or buy wallpaper—or do both! She could buy Ralph one of those big white Victorian cages with the graceful cupolas on the top. And Hunka and Munka could have velveteen cat beds and eat fresh chopped liver into the next century. Maybe she could get a saltwater aquarium with fish that would get along and not eat one another, as had happened when she was a teenager. God and all the angels in heaven had smiled on her!

"What do I have to do?" she asked, not caring if she had to walk barefoot through burning nettles.

Greely furrowed his brow. He leaned forward, all seriousness. "That's highly confidential. I'm afraid your service to Mr. Matthison can only be revealed by Mr. Matthison himself."

"I see," she said with the same tone of gravity. Clearly, when large sums of money were at issue, a certain dignity automatically asserted itself in the personalities of all concerned.

"Shall we go?" Greely rose before she had answered. The money must have spoken for her.

"Now?"

"Mr. Matthison is at home this afternoon, and it would be convenient if the matter can be resolved immediately. I'm sure you understand this sense of urgency, life and death situations being the basics of your business..."

"It does come up now and then...life and death," Cassandra said, thinking that was precisely what she hated about her line of work. Then she thought of Alex and of how worried she was about him. And then she thought of the forty thousand and all other thoughts were canceled out by the four zeros. "Am I okay this way?"

"Mr. Matthison is very casual at home. I'm sure you'll be appropriately dressed."

"Oh. Good." Actually, she was still dressed in her best two-piece suit. She grabbed her purse, locked all the doors and was off.

It was her first ride in a limousine. It was a hermetic environment, fit for killers or kings, Cassandra thought. The windows were tinted gray. The upholstery was a slate-colored plush fabric. The carpeting was deep and of the same dark hue. There was a small bar, a television set and what appeared to be a sophisticated telecommunications center built into the wall separating the driver's compartment from that of the passengers'.

Alan Greely didn't speak with her during the ride, though he did make a call, apparently to the Matthison estate, informing someone that they were in transit. The driver and the other man she had seen beside the limo were in front of a glass plate, and although they spoke a few times, the compartments were soundproofed. In terms of psychic vibrations, it was a very weird and uncomfortable drive.

Cassandra didn't know if her feelings of unease were due to being out of her socioeconomic element, or because there was, in fact, something not quite right about the scene she had entered.

But Philip Matthison was a public figure. Philip Matthison wasn't going to muck around in any kind of off-the-wall sordidness that could ruin him. She hoped, anyway. Certainly the men who worked for him dressed well.

They took the freeway, then surface streets, and arrived eventually at the private gate to Hidden Hills. The development was an enclave of multimillion-dollar estates belonging to movie stars and West Coast financial wizards and, some said, those members of the Cosa Nostra who wore suits instead of guns.

There were long low fences behind which horses grazed. There were Olympic-sized swimming pools in front yards, tennis courts off to the side and what might be fleets of Mercedes-Benzes, if counted altogether, parked in circular drives. There were teenagers in hundred-thousand-dollar foreign sports cars whizzing past, and a woman in a maid's cap driving a new Cadillac.

It was all kind of dazzling in an excessive sort of way. There was this sense of things having gotten out of control. There was the basic natural element: rolling land and lots of big trees, a kind of rural scrubbiness that brought to mind plain folk just out to live life as it was. But then there was all the other stuff, the pools and such. And except for the people whizzing past in cars, you never saw the plain folk. They weren't even swimming or batting balls back and forth, and certainly no plain folk could be seen gardening or feeding a horse. The whole idea seemed to represent God's idea of a compromise between Hollywood and ordinary reality. Maybe God had attended a meeting at the Polo Lounge and had lost final editing rights in this part of his production.

At last the journey came to a close. The limousine swept regally along a wide road that ended in the requisite circular drive at a sprawling white frame ranch house with a Grecian-style portico for an entrance.

Both doors of the limousine were opened, and Cassandra was helped from her side while Alan Greely left his and marched efficiently forward to the portico. Cassandra followed him, with the other two men remaining with the vehicle. Greely rang the bell once, and immediately the door swung open.

There was no conversation between Greely and the man who let them in, and Greely moved forward again, going down a wide central hall with a black-and-white marble floor. Cassandra followed.

At the end of the hall Greely stopped, looked briefly at Cassandra, almost smiled, and then rapped against one of the two double doors before him.

"Come," said a voice behind the wood.

Greely's hand moved to the handle, and the door opened to the most beautiful room Cassandra had ever seen. For openers, it was enormous. The walls were paneled in a rich honey-colored wood, over which hung an array of splendid paintings, ranging in style from Renaissance to abstract. An enormous hearth was at one end of the room, within which large logs crackled and sparked amid red and blue flames. The forest-green carpet was deep enough to twist one's ankles. The other predominant accent was red, appearing for the most part in leather furniture.

But perhaps the most impressive feature of the entire setting was the man who rose from behind a large antique desk. At the same time, a grandfather clock chimed the hour. It was four in the afternoon.

"Ah," the man said, "I'm glad our schedules meshed."

He didn't make a move toward them. Instead, Greely motioned her forward, making the verbal introductions as they approached.

"So," Philip Matthison said, his eyes as blue as the reports claimed, "I'm looking upon a woman who has the capability of killing a man twice her size."

"Actually, that's not the purpose of my art."

"Really? And what is the purpose?"

"It's actually more spiritually oriented. First and foremost, it combines the physical with the spiritual, and in this way it transcends the concept of life and death altogether."

"Perhaps you should have brought me a priest," Matthison quipped to Alan Greely. "No, not at all," he amended with a generous smile, "I'm sure you're exactly what I want. Please," he said, and offered her a chair. Alan Greely remained standing. Matthison seemed to forget his assistant was in the room as he continued to speak to Cassandra. "I, too, dislike violence for the sake of violence. Alas, some of my clients don't harbor this same sentiment, but . . ." He shrugged. The blue eyes seemed to pierce through Cassandra's scalp, seeking out her thoughts.

She had no thoughts. Her mind was in a state of such confusion that she could only catch a random word here and there in the hope of stringing several together to form a meaning. There was something not right about the situation.

Or so she thought until the hors d'oeuvres were delivered by a butler, and she had had two glasses of champagne, and Philip Matthison had taken her on a tour of the house, and his blue eyes had entered her mind, her body, her heart, and vaguely, she had come to consider herself, as is said . . . enchanted.

"So," Matthison said, leading her into what he referred to as his game room, "what do you think of my little place so far?"

"I'm enchanted," she said. "I mean, it's quite enchanting."

He smiled down at her as he opened the door to the game room. "Everything here means something. Nothing's random."

She had expected chess and checkers, a pool table or two, some electronic video games. She was mistaken. All over the walls were the mounted heads of animals, beasts felled in hunting expeditions—as evidenced by accompanying photos of the animals in their wholly embodied states, Matthison standing triumphantly by with weapon in hand. In one corner was an actual full-sized stuffed horse.

Matthison, alert to her curiosity, answered the silent question. "He was my first horse. My first friend."

"Oh," Cassandra said.

"His name was Devil."

"Oh," Cassandra said. She looked away from the animal's false, shining eyes. The setting was distasteful, macabre and violent. It was difficult to connect the charming man at her side with this room. Nor did this room seem to belong to the rest of the house. It was as if she had been admitted into some murky lower-level environment existing beneath the surface gloss of both man and building.

Even though dulcet tones continued to flow from Matthison's diaphragm and honeyed words dripped from his tongue, something was spoiled for her.

"I'll ring for some more wine," he said, walking to the desk.

"No," Cassandra said. "I'd like to leave, please."

Matthison paused, his finger not quite on the button he was to have pressed. "Certainly. We can have drinks in the—"

"I mean, I want to go home," Cassandra clarified. She felt very strongly about that, and it could be heard in her voice. Her mind was no longer confused. The eyes of the dead animals surrounding them had cleared her mind. Perhaps they, like she, had sensed danger, only it had been too late to run for safety.

"I'm sorry. That's not possible yet. Our business hasn't been concluded, Miss Burke."

For the first time since she had arrived, the electric-blue eyes of Philip Matthison didn't caress and dance across her soul when he gazed upon her. They sent a chill rocketing along her spine.

Chapter Thirteen

All the way to the desert, Alex kept seeing the face of Cassandra Burke in his mind. When he wasn't seeing her face, he was feeling her body as he had known it on those three occasions when they had—

He paused, arranging his mind around the feeling that arose full-strength from a region of himself that could never be diagrammed in *Gray's Anatomy*. The piece of him that held the smell, the touch, the taste of Cassandra Burke existed in a place that could not be found by medical science, yet it alone would never disappear as his body one day would.

To complete his sentence—when they had made love.

So there it was. *Love,* dammit.

He had truly fallen in love with the woman. How had it happened, and why, and when? With all his might he tried to think back to the exact time love had stolen into the picture. He followed each of their meetings back farther and farther, as if unraveling a string with the answer written somewhere along its length.

The thread continued to unwind until there was nothing left to it. He had reached the end of their experiences together, right to that first day they had met. And that, he realized with sudden clarity, was the beginning of it, right then and there. He saw it all, in a brilliant freeze-framed explosion of the mind: he, standing across the street, staring at the sign over the ordinary storefront; he, in the large room with the white-suited students standing on one leg; and the voice, clear and . . . and *hers*.

Reliving it all now, he heard the laughter of Fate in that moment. He heard the rustle of Destiny follow in his footsteps as he moved into her small, spare office. In the midst of the most ordinary sights and sounds, miracles were being woven into the fabric of life. How utterly fantastic life was.

Once he had thought he would never love again. When the thing with Samantha had ended, he had been left with a hole in him wider than the Grand Canyon and Rio Grande combined. Once he had thought only of making good on the engine, and there was no future beyond that one idea. It was as if his life ended where his imagination stopped. But now his thoughts raced, running so fast ahead of him he could barely follow. Crazy-quilt images of Cassandra and him shopping for furniture and working together to lay tile in a bathroom! Breakfast scenes. Raking-leaves-together scenes. Other, more exotic forms of the future slipped into his mind. There were moonlit boat rides in gondolas, and picnics in bed, and scenes in which they were running hand in hand through fields of flowers, and then there they were suddenly in another location, lying unclothed in the waves, their bodies joined together. He recognized some of the mini-dramas as direct plagiarizations of television commercials or vignettes borrowed straight from old movies. So what? Originality wasn't the point here. Desire and hope blotted out all trespasses against art. True love gave one the license to leap tall buildings and steal lines from famous poets.

As he drove, the very air he breathed seemed filled with sonnets. His heart swelled, tears rising of their own accord in his gratefulness to be alive and able to love again.

It was as if the engine was fueled by his euphoria, and the journey to the shack seemed to be made in a blink. He was living life in dream time now.

At the shack, he examined the Fiat and found it could be pieced back into running condition. He would stop by a body shop on the way out and give them instructions to haul the car off and do what it took to get it up on its wheels again. He had some money left for a few such disasters. Naturally he'd pay the whole thing himself—plus throw in a paint job. Alex imagined Cassandra's face when the car came rolling into view, all spiffed up, gleaming in the sunlight. When she smiled, it made his heart burst with a gladness of its own.

It took him no more than an hour to load up the car with his tools and the few personal belongings he could salvage from the fire. Some of the things had to be cleaned, covered as they were by cinder and dust. He worked feverishly to accomplish everything; the desire to rush back to Los Angeles was in the back of his mind constantly.

He had one other, unrelated piece of business to attend to. Retrieving the gun dropped by the men in the black van from the old tool chest beneath his bed, Alex took it to the well behind the shack. It was amazing how heavy such a small item could be. It was amazing how such a small item could shatter lives, not to mention whole worlds.

He looked down into the well, considering if he was wise to throw it away. Then he looked up into the sky. The serenity in the desert was like a long note, strained and holding. When a bird cried overhead, it jarred the atmosphere. Alex imagined the air vibrating around him, and then the single lonely note resumed.

He threw the gun into the well and waited. Much later he heard it hit bottom with a dull thud.

When he climbed back into the car he was tired yet exhilarated. There was something to look forward to at the end of the drive. There would be Cassandra and their dinner out together. Happily he projected his mind toward the evening.

He was a half hour out of town when a flash of light appeared in his side mirror. Alex's attention broke from his latest fantasy and watched as a black van drew up fast behind him. A collage of his whole life, from beginning to end, spun out before him in a single second. He was going to die. Cassandra...Cassandra. Her name was a howl through his soul.

But the van only tailed him for a few feet, then rushed ahead, passing him on the side. A woman with a small child crawling over her lap looked down at him through the window.

He wasn't going to die after all. Not yet anyway.

The traffic was snarled something fierce at the Los Angeles interchange. On the radio, news bulletins announced a plane crash somewhere in the Orient, and Alex thought of Og, as Cassandra called him. Yes, he wondered about Og. To inspire such blind allegiance, Og had to be some kind of a guy, in spite of his somewhat unorthodox behavior.

The Los Angeles gridlock was finally cleared, and twenty minutes later Alex found himself driving down

Twenty-third Street with the proverbial song in his heart and wings on his wheels, if not on his heels.

Lost as he was in his continuing fantasies, he hadn't been paying too much attention to what was going on in the outside world, but even he couldn't fail to notice the endlessly long white limousine pulling away from the curb in front of Cassandra's neighbor's house. No, he thought, leaning forward slightly, the limousine was pulling away from Cassandra's house.

Something in Alex resonated to a wrong vibration.

He stepped on the gas and made it into Cassandra's driveway just as the limo turned right, disappearing around the corner.

Alex leaped from the car, leaving the engine idling, and pounded on the front door. He rang the bell and called Cassandra's name.

As he had expected, there was no answer.

Rushing back to the car, he screeched out of the drive and took the corner on two wheels, his eyes intent on any sign of the white limousine.

He thought he'd lost the vehicle; then, on Cloverdale, it came into sight again, cruising like a giant marshmallow through traffic. Alex was a bus, a garbage truck, a Porsche and three old heaps behind when the limousine drifted onto the San Diego Freeway going north.

From behind the longest red light in the world, Alex watched it cruise swiftly away. Across from him two highway patrolmen sat in their black-and-white vehicle finishing doughnuts. In his mind, Rome burned.

The table was large. It was decorated as if for a party, with not one, but two large chandeliers dripping tear-shaped crystals overhead. The steady glow from the hanging fixtures bled into the spasmodic light cast by the flickering candles beneath. There were three dramatic flower arrangements positioned at equal intervals down the white damask-covered length of the table. The red and white blossoms, like the situation, didn't seem quite real to Cassandra. Even the two men, dressed in dark formal suits and standing unobtrusively against the wall, might have been wax figurines were it not for their eyes, which jumped at each unexpected sound, whether a cough or a spoon hit against a plate.

At the moment, food was being presented by a uniformed male servant. Cassandra watched as he glided with his silver platters and covered tureens from Philip Matthison, enthroned at one end of the table, to where she was seated at its far opposite side.

"The chateaubriand is excellent," Philip Matthison said to the servant. "Please tell Rogerio I compliment him."

"Thank you, sir."

Indeed, the beef might have been wonderful were Cassandra not sick to her soul with fright.

"Do you agree, Miss Burke?"

"Splendid," she said listlessly, picking at a green bean.

"There seems to be something wrong," Matthison said.

Cassandra raised her eyes and gave him her drop-dead look. "What do you want from me?" she asked.

"Your indispensable services."

"Which are?"

"At the moment? Merely to eat your dinner." Matthison motioned for more wine to be poured. "An excellent vintage," he announced, holding the glass up to the light of one of the chandeliers. "From the vineyard of one of my closest associates."

"The Mafia, no doubt," Cassandra mumbled.

"No doubt," Matthison said, smiling. "How perceptive are you, Miss Burke? How intelligent are you?"

"I'm smart enough to know I'm way over my head here," she replied. "But not smart enough to know what the hell you want with me."

"We have a mutual friend," Matthison said, savoring the wine's bouquet as he passed the glass near his nose.

"I doubt that."

"Oh, but we do. His name is Alex Montana. Or maybe you call him Rocky."

Cassandra's body grew as cold as the water glass she was holding. "Oh," she said feebly.

"Oh," Matthison echoed. "Now you get the idea?"

Cassandra stared back. "I think so. We're talking about making a deal. Like, am I supposed to do him in for you? Kind of a double cross? Is that it?"

"What a thought! Excellent, excellent..." Matthison applauded lightly.

"Well, I won't."

Matthison's brows shot up. "Oh, pity. Such a disappointment. Would you like more money?"

"No amount of money could possibly—"

"Fine. I so admire a woman of conviction."

"I'm ready to leave now," she said, throwing down her napkin. She rose from the chair.

Simultaneously the two men who had been standing against the wall sprang to life. Like magicians, they brought forth shiny black weapons from within their jackets. One man grabbed Cassandra by the arm. Her free arm was already in motion to disarm her attacker when the other man thrust the barrel of his weapon against her temple.

"Sit down, Miss Burke, and finish your dinner before it gets cold. If you're to be buried, let it not be on an empty stomach."

The man who held her arm thrust her roughly back into her seat.

Cassandra's pride was hurt, but that was all. Every lecture Og had ever given her resounded in her mind. Each move she had practiced under his tutelage flew before her. There was no way a few bozos in thousand-dollar suits were going to do in the number one disciple of Ogata Kenzo. Wherever Og was, he would know somehow, and he would never forgive her. Death was one matter; humiliation another. To die at the hands of this kind of lowlife certainly had no honor to it.

It was just too damn bad they had guns in their hands.

Cassandra picked up her wineglass, staring into it as if it were a crystal ball. What would Og do in a situation like this? she wondered. But of course that was easy. Og would never be so stupid as to get himself into such a mess. Once Og had told her he had been born in the year of the weasel.

An hour later she was still at the table. She was still thinking about what Og would do in her place. It was, however, becoming increasingly difficult to form any kind of coherent thought. Idly she wondered if there hadn't been a sedative in the wine. The room was becoming cloudy. Had the table become longer? Matthison appeared much farther away now.

At the present moment he was speaking on the telephone again. One of the servants had come with the remote device, whispering secretively into Matthison's left ear as the phone was offered. Whoever it was on the other end had to be someone significant. It was clear the dining ritual was important to Matthison, yet this caller took priority above the chocolate mousse over which Matthison had been waxing poetic.

When he put down the phone, he looked mildly troubled. It elevated Cassandra's spirits somewhat to think there might be a chink in her captor's armor.

"This is against the law," Cassandra said. "You can't keep me here against my will."

"I can do what I damn well please!" Matthison snapped. "I can do it, I will do it and I'll get away with it."

"There are laws—"

"Perhaps for other people. I'm above those laws," he said, and laughed unpleasantly, looking to his minions for confirmation.

A memory filled Cassandra's mind. Once Og had told her how everything in nature was balanced. There was a perfect law to life that superceded any of those efforts and acts designed by mortals to mete out their own forms of justice. It sounded good at the time, but as she faced Matthison she was pretty certain there was going to be an exception to Og's great cosmic rule. Matthison was going to beat the law of the universe.

At that very moment a terrible crashing sound filled the atmosphere. A lawn chair flew through the large dining room window, toppling the wooden frame with its panes of glass.

The well-dressed guards had drawn their weapons, but otherwise appeared as stunned as Cassandra and Matthison, who had leaped from his seat and was backing quickly toward the door.

No one was prepared for what came next. No one. How could anyone have dreamed it could happen?

In what seemed to be slow motion, the front end of a white horse flowed in through the empty hole where the window had recently been. Then came Alex Montana, astride the animal's bare back. At once the scene speeded into a crazy double-time action sequence.

All about there were exclamations of surprise and a lot of expletives interspersed with unintelligible but obviously heartfelt gasps and shouts. Pandemonium reigned.

Probably someone would have been killed, but at first no one could figure out how a horse and its wild rider had suddenly joined the flowers as a centerpiece.

Cassandra herself was unable to do more than gape in astonishment as Alex, wild-eyed and shouting like a banshee, charged about the room on horseback, twirling a rope and kicking at weapons, men and anything else in his path.

"Cassandra, up! Up!" Alex yelled, grabbing her beneath one arm and lifting her until she was pressed against the side of the snorting, neighing white beast.

Her arms aching and the chocolate mousse beginning to rise threateningly from the pit of her stomach, she was whirled around in circles and jolted high into the air as the animal bucked about the room.

Two weapons flew in opposite directions. Matthison was screaming at his men. A man with a chef's hat poked his head in, shrieked in Spanish and took off. Then as she was spun about, the view changed to Matthison in the midst of escaping from the room. He never made it. Alex's rope whistled through the air like a singing snake. It dropped over Matthison's head and coiled downward until the noose was closed tightly over his arms.

Matthison shouted, in pain and panic and rage, for help. None came. His pals were scrambling for safety beneath the table, nursing their aching sides and stomped-upon hands. Cassandra wasn't feeling too terrific herself. She was afraid parts of her anatomy were being dislodged from their sockets.

The wild ride continued. At least Alex seemed ecstatic, making his cowboy calls astride the horse, which snorted and ripped freely around the room. Cassandra clung to him. Mostly she whimpered and battled down the mousse.

Alex pulled on the rope holding Matthison and began backing out of the window—but not without some difficulty. The horse wasn't as accommodating in reverse as in forward.

"I'm going to kill you for this!" Matthison shouted as best he could. Just as in one of those old cowboy movies, he was being dragged across the ground.

"Later!" Alex called, and gave the rope a hard jerk.

Matthison went sailing forward, straight out the window with them. Cassandra heard a sudden "Ooooph!" Then there was a thud, followed by Alex's laugh.

Alex dropped the rope and Matthison along with it. "Climb up," he commanded Cassandra, then helped her settle behind him. "Hold on and don't let go," he ordered. "No matter what."

The scenery flashed by them in a blur as Alex raced over the bucolic terrain of Hidden Hills. They dashed through yards, narrowly avoiding plunges into swimming pools, leaped fences, scrabbled over driveways, crashed through patios. All the while, Cassandra held on to Alex's waist, her face pressed against his back, whispering prayers and whimpering in fear.

"Couldn't we take the road?" she shouted, all her joints rattling in different harmonies, directions and degrees of pain.

"No way." Alex pointed to the side. Cassandra saw the gleam of fast-moving headlights. "That's them. They can't jump fences. We can." And they did, a rather high one.

Just when Cassandra thought she would die from fright or physical deterioration, the ride came to an end.

The peace, after the thunder of horse hooves, was almost deafening to her ears as Alex slipped her to the ground. He followed after, giving their white charger a slap to its flanks and setting it off on its way.

"Come on," he said before she could catch her breath. "The car's over there."

Now on a run by foot, they scaled a low wall separating Hidden Hills from the ordinary world.

"You know," Cassandra said breathlessly as they made a dash for Alex's car, which was parked on the road across from the gate, "you'll never be invited there for dinner again."

Chapter Fourteen

An hour later—or maybe, as it seemed, a lifetime later—Cassandra sat on the edge of Alex's bed in his motel room. She held her head between her hands and shook it back and forth. "Do you hear ringing?" she asked.

"Like a high-pitched whine?"

"Yes," Cassandra said with relief. It was always comforting to share a malady.

"No."

"No?" She looked at him in bewilderment. "But you just described—"

"Forget it," he said. "I was just trying not to talk about real stuff."

"Right now the ringing is pretty damn real, Alex."

"It'll stop," he said offhandedly. During their conversation, he had been pacing the short length of the room. Now he came to a halt before her and said, "How could you be so dumb? Cassandra, for a smart woman you sometimes seem . . .'' He sighed. "Beyond naive.''

"Philip Matthison's a big cheese. He's major establishment. How was I to know Matthison had any connection with those guys who're trying to do us in?" After she said it, she realized she had spoken in the plural rather than the singular. It was a big self-admission, and it didn't sit any better in her than the chocolate mousse. "They were going to pay me enough to save my house, and then some. Anyway," she said, feeling magnanimous in spite of the insult, "I'm glad you turned up to save my skin."

Alex was rubbing his shoulder. "Don't remind me about skin," he said.

Cassandra kicked off her shoes and moved back on the bed, positioning herself against the headboard. "Why would someone like Matthison be involved with people like us? I mean, we're kind of penny-ante, aren't we?"

"I imagine Matthison hangs out with the big boys, all right. But some of them didn't get to be big boys by playing fair. I'm sure Matthison could care less, personally, about me and my engine. But someone else does. And he probably works for that someone. Or owes them a favor."

"I think they wanted me to kill you."

"No, they wouldn't have trusted you."

"Why?" she said, insulted. "I like money. Why couldn't I be bought like the rest of the world? And these hands are lethal weapons, remember?"

"You're only a woman." He quickly smiled. "No, they probably figured I'd be willing to swap the engine for your safety."

"Of course you wouldn't," Cassandra said, but found herself watching for signs to the contrary.

"No way. I mean, if you had been something great, like a horse or a terrific prize steer, then we might be talking a deal."

Cassandra threw the pillow at him.

"What do you think?" he said, coming over to the bed and sitting down. "You think I did that whole scene in the dining room because I felt like taking a gallop through a dinner party?"

"Knowing you—"

"Yeah, well, you don't know me." He was quiet for a while, looking from her to his knuckles, which were raw and crisscrossed with tiny cuts. "Even I don't know me anymore." He jumped up suddenly and picked up the phone. "You like pizza?" he asked.

"Now?"

"Why not?"

"Because I may be sick if I see any more food tonight."

"I've gotta eat," he said, and went about ordering a pizza to be delivered.

Forty minutes later they had an Italian picnic in the middle of the bed. Cassandra even ate half a piece, so rapt was she in the horse drama related by Alex between mouthfuls of deep-dish Chicago-style crusty decadence.

Alex thought he had lost the limousine, but as luck would have it, he found it on the freeway, stranded temporarily behind a truck that had lost its load of women's panty hose across two lanes. Politely Alex had allowed the limousine to glide in front of him and managed to tail it through the traffic, maintaining a discreet distance naturally. At the gate to Hidden Hills, Alex was stopped cold by the guard. It took some conversational gymnastics, but he was able to find out that the white limousine belonged to Matthison.

"The white horse was a nice touch," Cassandra complimented. "Dashing."

"Thank you. It was at that." Alex nodded in agreement, obviously savoring the memory of the rescue. "Especially since it belonged to Matthison." He grinned.

"I could love you," Cassandra said suddenly. "Maybe. Someday," she qualified. "If both of us were to live that long."

Alex had just bitten into another slice of pizza. A portion of a pepperoni was just disappearing. It stopped halfway into his mouth. "Ummm...?" he mumbled.

"It could happen," Cassandra said casually. She closed her eyes, dreading the new foolishness she was embarking upon. "I realized it tonight when I saw you come flying through the window on that horse. I always knew I'd fall in love with a man on a white horse. I just thought he'd be...different."

She opened her eyes then. Alex was staring at her. The pepperoni was gone.

Alex said nothing. He barely took his eyes from her but managed to move the napkins, pizza box and paper plates to the floor, then in a single fluid motion pulled her down flat on the bed.

"Woman," he said, bringing his body over hers, "I never expected to be a man on a white horse. And I certainly never expected you..."

Her mouth opened to his, and body and soul, she felt their two lives becoming one. "I didn't say I loved you...I only said I might...someday..."

"I didn't say I loved you, either. But I'm willing to pretend if you are."

"Just for now," Cassandra sighed.

"Why the hell not?"

They made love slowly once; and the second time with more passion. Later, Alex woke her to tell her he, too, felt that someday he might be able to love her more than the engine and all the horses and cows he had ever known, and for a third time their bodies united.

In the morning they stayed in bed past noon. Finally they both managed to groan their way out of bed.

"How do you know if every bone in your body has been broken?" Cassandra asked, shuffling off to shower.

"Parts of you drop off as you move about," Alex said. "Yick..."

"Spare yourself the horror. Just don't look back. You won't know if anything's missing."

When she came out of the shower, Alex went in.

He hadn't been in for thirty seconds when he called out for her. His voice was urgent. Alarmed, Cassandra rushed in, only to be snatched into the stall.

"Alex..." she sputtered, the water racing over her face as his tongue probed her body. "Alex... please, no. Oh, that... Alex."

"Maybe this'll be more comfortable." He pulled her down to the floor, ran soapy fingers along her breasts and neck and stomach, down along her thighs and between her legs, until the water beating down like needles became no more to her than the soft patter of spring rain.

She had never made love in the rain before, but it couldn't have been better than feeling Alex, hard and slippery, moving against and finally into her.

"Say it again," he said, their bodies joined.

"Ummm, what?" Cassandra murmured, barely able to form words in her mind.

"What you said before... about the man on the white horse."

"I...could...love...him," she said, her eyes open now, water running in currents off her forehead and down her face.

"Good ... good ..." Alex said, pressing into her more deeply. "Good ..." he said, and his eyes closed as she slowly rotated against him, bonding their bodies together. "Maybe someday I could love a woman like you, too."

Alex pulled up before her house. His face was arranged into a mask of worried disapproval.

"Just get the animals fed. You're going to stay with me," he said, grabbing her hand before she could slide out the door.

Cassandra sighed, and turned to give him her own long-suffering look. "I can't, Alex. I have obligations of my own. I told you. I've got to find a job. I've got to think of some way to save my house from foreclosure. I've got the animals and mail. I've got a whole life to go on with."

"Are you crazy, or what?" Alex said.

"Look, I was stupid before," she admitted. "But that's because I didn't know exactly what I was up against. Now's different. Now I know not to trust smiling men in sharkskin suits. They turn out to be sharks. Okay? Satisfied?"

"I don't like it," Alex said.

"I don't like it, either," Cassandra agreed morosely. "But it's not like I'm incapable of defending myself. Og taught me good," she quipped.

"Oh, yeah," he said. "You certainly handled things well over at Matthison's."

"They had guns! Give me a break!"

"I just want you to know something." He looked at her seriously. She looked back just as seriously. "I don't have another white horse at my disposal. The next time you get yourself into a mess, it could be the last. You got that?"

"It computes."

"Good." He sighed in frustration, then hit the steering wheel hard with one hand. "So, I've got some banking to take care of or this baby's going to be running on air soon. It's good, but not that good."

"Maybe we could get together later," Cassandra said.

Alex looked at her, understanding she was making a major social overture. "Sure. We can relive old war stories."

They both knew it was important to keep things light.

"Exactly what I had in mind," Cassandra said.

"Chinese food at six?"

"In or out?"

"I strongly suggest we eat at home."

"You think it's dangerous?" Cassandra asked in alarm. Her world was becoming smaller with every day she knew Alex Montana.

"Not necessarily, but maybe. We'd be closer to the shower."

"That's vulgar and disgusting," she said, sticking her nose up in the air.

"Why? Cleanliness is next to godliness. Besides, you didn't think it was so out of line this morning."

"I was coerced," she said. "Manipulated. Maneuvered."

"You liked it."

Cassandra gave him a crooked smile. "So bring back some Chinese food."

Alex kissed her again, more deeply this time. It was hard for them to draw apart. It took five serious tries before Cassandra made it out the car door.

"See you..." they both said at the same time.

He waited until she was safely inside the house, then when she waved from the front window, signaling that all was well, he finally drove off.

But all was not entirely well.

In the refrigerator, for instance, there was something amiss with the orange juice. Specifically there was less in the plastic container than she had remembered when she had poured glasses for herself and Alex. Severe condensation?

And then there was the bowl that was out of place in the cupboard. She had this thing about her bowls. She liked to rotate the colors in order. If she used the blue bowl, she put it on the bottom, so the next time she would give the pink bowl a chance to shine. It might have been stupid, but that's the way it was. She imagined bowls having feelings, just as she imagined weeds being really nice plants who had been given a bad rap.

Her blue bowl was out of position.

But who would come into her house and drink her orange juice and shuffle her bowls around? Some health food bowl freak?

She did a tour of the rest of the house. Nothing else appeared out of place. Nothing was stolen, at least not that she could determine. The doors and windows were all secure. The only explanation could be that she must have been distracted when Alex was there and varied her routine with the bowls, forgot about the juice. Nothing, now that Alex was in her life, was routine anymore.

A half hour before Alex was to arrive, everything was ready. She had picked up a bottle of Chinese plum wine from the market and set it on the table to chill in a silver bucket. There were flowers, too, although nothing elaborate—just a mixed bouquet, also from the grocer's. But they looked gay, the myriad colors enlivening the room, and Cassandra knew Alex would appreciate the touch. There was something basically romantic and observant about him. Both qualities were a surprise to her, totally unexpected traits from a man who had once, and not long ago, bumped along on the backs of steers.

At six o'clock she was waiting for the sound of his car. At six-thirty she was beginning to be piqued that he wasn't on time. By seven o'clock she was worried. And by eight o'clock she was frantic.

The most terrible scenes flashed through her mind.

What if she never saw him again? What if their good-bye in the car that afternoon had been the last time they would ever see each other? He could be dead, even now. Or, she thought, finding that idea too horrible to contemplate for long, perhaps he was absolutely fine, but after thinking about their relationship, had decided that it was just too painful and complicated to pursue. By not showing up, he might be making a clean break of the whole thing. Sometimes that was the only way—just to end it. Eventually both parties would come to some deep, inner understanding that this was the only way things could have ever been.

Hadn't she seen films like that, read books, in which the public was led to understand—in retrospect—that the way things turned out had to be? The seeds of destiny had been planted way back in the couple's first meeting. There would always be a flashback to a flag waving just so, or the sound of a train's lonely whistle. What was once perceived as no more than an inconsequential image would now be seen as immensely meaningful and tragic.

Cassandra racked her mind for some such image in her own situation but couldn't narrow anything down that could close a film satisfactorily. She hoped her failure to do so might constitute some sort of positive omen.

She called Alex at the motel, but there was no answer. She left a message and got no return call.

At midnight she crawled into bed with the bottle of plum wine, still listening for the sound of his knock. It never came. Somehow she must have dozed off.

In the morning she awoke, and for a brief instant it might have been any other day. Old impulses traveled through her on automatic pilot. She would get up, get dressed, take care of the animals, drive to the studio—

But in the next instant she knew that all of this had been wiped away. Past history.

And in the next instant she remembered Alex. Present tense.

Eventually she did get up, but only to slop through the house in her pink robe and fuzzy yellow slippers. The table was still set from the night before. She stopped in the middle of her tracks and stared at it as if looking back on some page in a history book showing the site of a lost civilization. There had been people here once, folks, and then they were gone, disappeared. Just like that. How? Why? Was there any meaning to any of it? How were the lives of these people touched? How was the course of history changed? Did it matter if the course of history was changed?

All at once she missed Og. She missed him tremendously with an enormous ache. In a way, Og had been her soul's torment, but he had also been her mentor and a good friend when push came to shove. That's what made his running out on her hurt so much. It was the ultimate betrayal because it was so unexpected. But Og could have answered her questions about lost civilizations, and table arrangements. If anyone knew about the meaning of life, it was Og. She didn't know how he knew, only that behind his sparkling, often shifty black eyes, lay a whole heap of wisdom.

Ralph was batting around in his cage. Shuffling over in her slippers, she took off the cover.

"Greetings, bird," she said, sticking her nose close to the metal bars and peering in at Ralph. "I am the Bird Cage Goddess come to banish dark and bring you light. Arise, arise and chirp, twirp." But Ralph was out of sorts and only stared back at her from the other side of the bars. It was going to be that kind of day.

She left Ralph to brood, flippered her way into the kitchen and started a kettle of hot water for coffee. Hunka and Munka had not yet returned from their nocturnal socializing. The house was quiet, too quiet, she thought, as she went back through the living room into the foyer and outside to fetch her newspaper.

In the kitchen again she threw the paper on the table and went about mixing a cup of instant coffee for herself before sitting down and examining the day's fresh quota of disasters.

Maybe she could keep her mind off of Alex.

On page one: another uprising in a South American country; another revolt in Ireland; a cry for future vengeance of past crimes in the Middle East by two warring factions with initials for names; something terrible in India again. Nothing new.

Page two: Oh. Princess Di designed her own hat. That was nice. Ah, and the famous bug suit had finally been settled. Good, and certainly about time. A roach had been discovered floating feelers-up in the soup of a famous movie star dining in a famous restaurant. The famous movie star had gone into a deep depression over the incident and was subsequently unable to fulfill her contractual obligations with a motion picture studio. She had been hired to play the starring role in a remake of *The Fly*—only from the female viewpoint. It was apparently all she could do to mope her way to the witness stand and relate the horror of the experience to the jurors. It was a trip for naught. In essence, the jurors said the whole incident should be considered bug soup under the bridge and gave her nothing. Well, well, Cassandra thought, nodding, all was not lost in this world after all.

Page three: lots of boring stuff and a story about . . . no, it couldn't be. But it was. She read on, the print burning into her soul.

Charlie Otis, the legendary oilman, otherwise known as Big Charlie, who had at one time been among the ten richest men in America and whose fortunes had plummeted to almost nothing during the 1973 energy crisis, had been felled the previous afternoon while eating Italian food. The cause of death was as yet unverified, but it was known that Charlie Otis had grave intestinal problems brought on by his oversized girth. It was speculated by friends and those of the medical profession that Charlie's insides had finally just given up the ghost.

Cassandra let the paper fall into her lap. She stared at the wall. They were wrong of course. It wasn't Charlie's appetite that had done him in: it was obviously the Mafia who had gotten him. How perfect. A surprise execution, perhaps done with poison. And all along Charlie had been convinced it was Detroit and the Arabs who were out to get him. God, Cassandra thought, for all she knew it could have been all of them working together.

Poor Jerry and now Big Charlie, and where was Alex?

She was morosely pondering the question, wishing for the thousandth time that she hadn't been so harsh during their times together, when the doorbell rang.

Chapter Fifteen

He was about seventeen years old, tall and skinny, with blue eyes and braces. He smiled uncertainly as he said, "Delivery for Miss Burke?"

With a heart that had already bottomed out, Cassandra took the envelope. If no news was good news, any news had to be bad news. Something from the bank to brighten up her life, no doubt. She could already imagine the opening sentence: *We hereby inform you that under the terms and conditions of such and such, we are hereby exercising our right to ruin your day, destroy your life and make you cry for years to come... if you should even live so long.*

Closing the door, she leaned against its solid support and tore open the white envelope bearing her name. Instead of a summons to appear in debtors' court, or a threat of having her roof removed from above her head, she found a ticket to Reno, Nevada, and a paid reservation at the

Sheraton Hotel. The travel agency's number was printed on an attached computerized form. She called and asked for the Judy who had put through the order.

"I think it's very nice, but I'd really like to know who to thank for this trip," Cassandra said.

Judy checked her file. "'Rocky,' it says here."

"Oh, Rocky...yes. Well, thanks."

Alex was all right! Her heart revived. It shot up sparkling, right out of the morbid depths of despair.

Soon they'd be together again, and everything—everything was now going to be different. For one thing, she'd declare herself emotionally. Oh, maybe not go the entire way—there was such a thing as being rash—but she'd lay a certain number of cards down on the table. She'd let him know she was really in love with him—she was, she was!—but, of course, that didn't necessarily mean she was ready for the altar, or anything permanent like that. Of course, she thought, as she raced to the bedroom, he might not be ready either.

It took her a half hour to pack and dress, five minutes to take care of Ralph and make sure the cats had food, one minute to lock up and fifteen seconds to get into the cab that arrived exactly on time. Happiness could make a lot of things possible. But love could even make a disorganized person efficient.

Los Angeles International Airport was jammed. People who appeared to know what they were about moved like clever eels through the crowd. Others, wearing bewildered expressions, trundled along with parcels and luggage and relatives, squinting uncertainly at signs telling them where to stand or not stand.

Cassandra selected a check-in line, basing her decision on the faces of people already waiting there. They appeared intelligent, their bodies more streamlined, auguring swiftness.

She was wrong of course. A man at the head of the line she had chosen was angry about something. She waited. Supervisor after supervisor came to reason and explain the airline's side of the situation. The other lines moved steadily forward.

Cassandra tried to figure the success odds on changing to another location, or sticking it out where she was. Finally she moved two lines down and took a place behind a small old woman who looked neither streetwise nor fleet of foot.

She noticed another man behind her also make the same decision. The reason she noted him amid all the swirling activity was that he was dressed so well. He had on a dark suit, white shirt, nice paisley tie and carried an expensive attaché case. Fashionable as his ensemble might have been aesthetically, from an emotional perspective, Cassandra didn't find him a particularly fetching sight. The sartorial elegance brought to mind Alan Greely and the rest of the Matthison contingent.

Her new line also dawdled along. A woman's suitcase, packed to the brim, burst its hinges and spewed forth mountainous layers of skirts, shoes and sweaters. It was an amazing sight, and brought forth gasps of despair and astonishment from those who observed an entire boutique spring forth on the baggage weighing scale.

Eventually Cassandra managed to inch her way to the front of the line. She figured she could have flown to Europe and back in the time it took her to get her seat assignment. The carry-on bag didn't need to be checked. Dragging it after her, she made her way up to the departure area.

There was still time until takeoff. Pulsing with happy anticipation, she looked for something to do to keep her mind off her meeting with Alex. There were restaurants, bars and convenience shops scattered around the perimeter of the gate area. She could browse. Also she wanted a magazine to read, and then remembered gum would be good to help keep her ears from hurting during the altitude changes. As she paid for her purchases, she glanced up and saw the man in the fashionable suit eyeing her. She had been eyed a time or two in her life, of course, and made little of the attention. It merely went with the territory of being an attractive woman.

Then, when she sat down to wait for the flight to be called, she noted him standing off to the side, again watching her. This time when their eyes met, he quickly raised a newspaper and covered his face.

Cassandra felt a warning chill pass up her spine. Lifting her bag, she moved casually off to one of the concessions selling juice and sandwiches. From the corner of her eye, she could see the man alter his position. Slowly— stealthily—he made his way toward her location.

This was no coincidence. She took a tray from the counter and pushed it along the stainless steel, pretending to ponder ham and cheese versus turkey on white. Her arm ached. Balancing the carryon and her purse in the crook of one arm was no easy feat.

The man following her didn't look as if he belonged to the ranks of the common masher. And, granted, she might exude a certain attractiveness to the opposite sex, she still didn't think her physical attributes would provoke a well-dressed man to skulk through an airport just to get a better view of her profile. Highly romantic, and even more highly unlikely.

There was one way to be sure, however.

She abandoned the tray and sped through the service line and back into the airport proper. The terminal was divided into two huge wings, with the concessions separating the different lounge areas, off which were located the gates. Rather than return to the lounge she had left, she walked to the other wing and took a seat. She waited.

But not long. Ten seconds passed, and the man was there again. This time he was behind the newspaper, his back against a wall. It was definitely him. She could tell by his shoes and the gold watch gleaming from where his raised cuff fell back into his jacket sleeve.

Hastily she picked up her carryon once again. This time she moved as fast as she could, trying to disappear into a crowd of Japanese tourists. Los Angeles International was the third busiest airport in the world, a comforting statistic in her present circumstance. Glancing back, she saw the man traveling after her at good clip, and then, extraordinarily, she caught a blur of another man. The second man's impression was no more than an optical blip before he literally disappeared from sight.

Her nervous system sounded a second note of alarm.

This was serious. This wasn't some stuff that was going to go away when she did. Her pursuers were obviously equipped to follow her to Reno or, if need be, to the far ends of the earth.

Cassandra came out of her thoughts long enough to find herself staring down the up escalator.

If she took an escalator, they'd be on it, too. They were going right along with her on that plane, and when they did catch up with her, she doubted they were going to be delivering singing telegrams to her hotel room. Obviously it wasn't Alex who had sent her the ticket to Reno.

Alex ... Alex ... where was he? Was he still alive? Oh, Alex ... be alive, my darling ... please. A tear squeezed itself from the corner of her eye.

First Jerry. Then Big Charlie. And Alex...? No, no. She wouldn't allow herself to add Alex's name to the hit list. A man who could save a damsel in distress on the back of a white horse simply couldn't go the way of an ordinary flesh-and-blood victim.

But she didn't count herself a member of Alex's mythic league. She was definitely vulnerable—not to mention popular. The man in the black suit was suddenly there behind her again, his head bobbing above the members of the Japanese tour group.

Maybe it was confusion, perhaps genius, but she suddenly bolted down the up escalator. The man in the black suit was clever, too. Or so he thought. Instead of following her, he rode the down conveyance, increasing his speed even more by descending two steps at a time. He was going at twice her rate. His face registered the satisfaction of a fox about to dine. She kept as close tabs on his progress as he did hers. Strangers no more, their eyes met frequently, in furtive, measuring glances.

She switched directions.

Up she went again, and now the man was scowling up at her from the bottom, waiting for a victim who was not to arrive.

Ha! Good for her, too bad for him!

However, he was already forcing his way up the escalator, roughly pushing people aside. Obviously clothes do not make the gentleman, Cassandra thought, also realizing there wasn't a lot of time to waste on her victory celebration.

Tearing through the upper terminal, she made a circular tour from one side to the other, watching for the second man, the blur in her vision. She caught him. Ah, but he was crafty. Dressed not in black but in gray, he darted off behind a post, seemingly dissolving into the air. She waited, but he never reappeared. Her main attention was then directed back to the escalator. And sure enough, there he was, Mr. Sartorial Splendor himself.

Off the moving steps he flew, and looking both ways, without catching sight of her, he took off in the opposite direction.

Cassandra skittered back to the down escalator again, keeping one eye open for signs of her pursuers.

Momentarily safe, she didn't know how to stay safe. The downstairs was even more crowded than before. That was something at least: safety in numbers. If the gods were momentarily with her, so also was half the world, it seemed, all packed into the one terminal. She angled her way through passengers, secure in the density, and tried to think above the din.

If the guys who were after her were part of the Matthison group, they knew her address. It would be crazy to return home now. Of course she didn't have much money on her; maybe thirty or forty dollars. She racked her mind for other immediately available resources. All she had was a ticket to Reno and a prepaid room at the Sheraton.

As she thought this, a man and woman with long dreadlocks passed by, looking like a carnival in full swing. The man, who was tall, strutted by in a cloak of red leather studded with silver bullet shells. The outfit was completed with high-heeled red boots and silver spandex pants, so tight you could almost see the veins in his legs. The woman was a competing vision in a jumpsuit comprised of silver parachute material and white boots overlaid with white feathers and silver sequins. A white pearl Egyptian-type headpiece was draped over her copious black dreadlocks.

Faint tinkling and swishing sounds produced by her costume accompanied each step she took. If Cleopatra had been an astronaut, she would have looked exactly like that, Cassandra thought, as she gawked at the duo along with everyone else within a hundred yards.

If the couple noticed or minded the stares of outrage and interest and amusement their presence generated, they didn't give any indication. With jaunty good humor etched on their faces, they took their places in a line designated for passengers going to Las Vegas.

And of course that was it. Trumpets might have blared. Skyrockets might have underlined the revelation. Las Vegas, Cassandra thought, Las Vegas!

"Excuse me," she said, sidling up to the flamboyant pair. There was hope here. If anyone was apt to buy her weird story, it would be them. "Strange as this may sound, there happen to be a couple of men here at this airport who are trying to kill me. This is not a joke, this is the truth."

"Hey, baby!" the man said with a wide smile, "I can dig that."

"Oh. Good. Because I'd appreciate it very much if you would take this ticket here—on the same airline—and trade it in for another one for Las Vegas. I'll be in the rest room over there—praying."

"Honey," said the woman, "we've had trouble on our tails a time or two ourselves."

"Pray no more," the man said, slipping the ticket into his red cloak. "They don't call me Marvis the Magnificent for nothin'."

"I'm serious," Cassandra said.

"So's he, honey, so's he."

Ten minutes passed. Then, in a flurry of white feathers and silver, Marvis's companion swept into the institutional beige environment, her presence lighting up the surroundings as well as Cassandra's life.

"You live long enough, honey, catch our act at the Silver Crescent."

"Oh, I will, I will," Cassandra promised, checking the ticket she had been handed. "What do you do?" she asked, partly out of curiosity and mostly out of politeness.

"Oh, mostly we look good. And we look weird. And sometimes we like to make out we're singers." She laughed.

God, Cassandra thought, to laugh like that again...

"Thanks," she said. "Really, this is just great. You really saved my life. Really. I wish there was something I could do to—"

"Ya'll just applaud. And Marvis don't mind no screams, neither, or clawing at his clothes. Me, I'm a mite bit more reserved. I'll settle for a simple thanks." She grinned and pranced out. The room was dimmer.

The few women in the room stared at Cassandra.

"A good friend of mine," Cassandra said. She meant it.

Everything started out okay in Vegas, and then just kept getting better and better. It was very weird, all this sudden good luck, and Cassandra couldn't help being highly suspicious of the curveball fate was pitching her way.

First of all, she had managed to evade the man in the black suit, and whoever else it was who was out to get her. Upon arrival in Vegas, she got her room at the Sheraton, using her prepaid voucher for Reno. After that, she ate in one of the buffets. Stuffed to the gills, and ten dollars lighter, she had intended to flop down on her bed and call it a day, when she passed a table where a perfectly ordinary-looking woman of around her own age was winning a perfectly extraordinary amount of money. Chips were piled up like treasure trove around a pirate. Along with a lot of other people, Cassandra stopped to watch. The woman lost a couple of rounds, wagered a stack on another hand, and lost that, too. Everyone sighed in disappointment, including Cassandra. There was something so satisfying in seeing one of "them" beat the "house."

When the woman rose, collecting her chips into a large leather purse, Cassandra slipped into the empty seat. She didn't know what made her do that. She hardly knew how to play the game, and adding numbers quickly wasn't high on her list of life's accomplishments.

She had help, however. The dealer jollied her along, and a man behind her seemed to know when she should ask for a card or stand her ground.

In less than twenty minutes she turned thirty dollars into three hundred and was shaking like a leaf. A cocktail waitress appeared and took an order for a glass of champagne. She drank it, and nourished by thousands of bubbles, she kept the balloon payment firmly in her mind's eye as she turned the three hundred into five hundred. By her third glass of champagne, her blood vibrated to the slap of cards against green felt. Each and every bubble had risen to her head. Her head was an enormous, weightless bubble, and she felt she was invincible. If someone had dared her, she could have swung from the chandeliers. If someone had asked her, she could have slain dragons or danced on tables or— In the midst of the euphoria, with her stack of chips before her, she thought of Alex. She thought of his lips on her body and his hands running along her legs. She thought of his smile, and his eyes crinkling at the corners, and the hard edge to his voice sometimes, as well as the soft vulnerability he hid beneath his exterior. She thought of him inside and out, upside and down, the taste, the smell, the feel of him, and all at once, she was sobbing.

"Hey, hey," the man behind her said, the one who had been helping her out. "You gotta back off a while, honey. Gambler's nerves gotcha."

Cassandra shook her head. "No...it's love that's got me. What if he's dead?" she asked, hardly able to see the man who was helping her off the stool.

He had collected her chips for her. "You wanna tip that guy something?"

"What?"

The man threw a chip the dealer's way, then opened Cassandra's purse to drop in her winnings, after which he carefully closed everything up. Cassandra was dimly aware she was being treated kindly, but couldn't quite get a secure fix on anything. Her head was a champagne bubble, about to drift into orbit.

"Lady luck's been good to you, honey. Now you be good to you, too. I'd pack it in, I were you."

"Thanks, thanks," Cassandra said with a sniffle. "I will. I'll just quit while I'm ahead." She began to laugh. "A head...I'm a head." She held her hand over her head, as if it were in lift-off position.

"Honey, you get yourself off to where you aren't going to be a danger to yourself or no one else."

"Ummm..." Cassandra said, the reference to danger having a definite sobering effect on her latest outburst.

She was unlocking her door minutes later. It was only 9:00 p.m. in one of the most exciting cities in the entire world and she was ready to pack it in.

Suddenly, as she entered the bright and unfamiliar hotel room, she didn't want to be alone. She didn't ever want to eat alone, or sleep alone, ever again.

And then, three steps into the room, the security lock in place, she realized something else. It was something terrible.

She had left the lights off. And she had not slept in her bed. But someone else had.

At that moment she knew how Goldilocks must have felt just before meeting the three bears. It wasn't good.

Chapter Sixteen

With his shirt off and his slacks on, Alex lay in yet another strange bed, in yet another strange town, feeling in every sense the reality of what he was: a man alone, a man whose every passing day seemed to bring with it more problems. Weary as he was, physically and mentally, he couldn't sleep. Sleep was less a physical necessity now than it was a necessary emotional withdrawal from all the confusing aspects of his life. He was his father's son after all.

It wasn't as if life had been tremendously easy in the past. Nevertheless, he had coped. But, as he looked down the length of the bed, he saw the long form of his body covered by the blue blanket and felt the weight of his present difficulties as being almost insurmountable. He had never been so anxious, so furious, so frightened—and so in love in his entire life. How all of these conflicting emotions could exist in one man, at one single time, was a mystery he knew he was never going to solve. Nevertheless, that was the way it was.

The woman had driven him wild with worry. It wasn't bad enough that he had to worry about his own neck? No. Now he had Cassandra's to consider as well.

But there was another element involved in all of this, too. That was the fact that he was also reveling in the responsibility of taking command of a situation again. As well as anxious, it made him feel powerful. There was a certain exhilaration to the prospect of taking care of someone he loved.

All of these thoughts and feelings ran together in one stream as he heard the sound of the hotel door opening. His body went into an alert mode.

There was no such thing as being too careful anymore. It might be Cassandra; then again, it could be almost anyone, especially someone he wouldn't want to see. These days there was no way of knowing when trouble was going to look him in the eye and spit.

With this in mind, he bounded from the bed where he had been hoping to rest and streaked for the bathroom where he could at least make a surprise attack if necessary.

He smelled her scent first, something flowery, bringing to mind summer fields and butterflies and the warmth of the sun on bare arms. Cassandra. A happiness filled him, a luxuriant smile expanding throughout his entire being, as he watched her pass by the door. His Cassandra...

So relieved was he, so gladdened at her presence, he even forgot the angry speech he had prepared for the occasion of their reunion as he stepped from the dark hollow of the bathroom and into the lighted hotel room.

The mellow feeling was short-lived.

As he moved forward, Cassandra whirled around and kicked him in the jaw.

Alex fell backward. With a thump, his head crashed against the door. For a moment the bright room, not to mention the rest of the world, was extinguished. Vaguely he could feel himself slither to the floor. Then, after who could tell how long a time, there was a flickering of light. He made a few feeble attempts to refocus and align himself with the rest of the universe. At last Cassandra's face swam into view. At the same time, her voice rushed from a hollow tunnel, and words began to surround and fill him. He was back again.

"Oh, Alex...oh, my love...my darling...you're alive, you're here, I'm so sorry..."

He broke into a smile, beginning to appreciate this channel he had tuned into, when abruptly it changed to: "You! How could you scare me like this! And where the hell were you all night? You promise me Chinese food, and deliver—"

"Surprises."

"Unpleasant ones."

"All fortune cookies don't promise paradise."

"I've had men trying to kill me while you've been—Where were you, Alex?"

It wasn't a question. It was a condemnation. He stared at her, wondering if it would be better to just throw her on the bed and make love to her for five hours, or fight like a man. He decided to do both, in reverse order.

"You want to complain, huh?"

"You better believe it."

"Fine, just fine. Complain away. But," he said, "just so you know, I've got my own ax to grind."

"Oh, really? For instance...?"

"For instance, why the hell can't you ever do what you're told to do? I had to move heaven, not to mention go through hell, to get a seat on that plane to Vegas. You want to know what happened to the Chinese food? I'd like to know what happened to Reno!"

That also wasn't a question, but an accusation.

Cassandra's eyes, which had been pinpricks of fury up to now, suddenly softened to concern. She reached up and touched his face lightly, just above the point where his jaw ached. The feel of her hands on his skin made his entire body shiver with desire, and something even more. A corresponding tenderness to protect her rose within him. Again he felt as if he wanted to throw her to the ground and thrust every pulsation of love into her...and hold her gently in his arms. Forever.

"It hurts?" she asked softly.

"Yeah," he affirmed. He meant something else entirely different from the physical pain of his body, though. A whole lot hurt him these days.

Cassandra, who was crouched down before him, rose and disappeared into the bathroom. When she came back, he was standing. She held out a cold washcloth, which she placed on his swelling jaw.

"Sorry. It's going to be a lump," she said.

"Colorful?"

"Very."

"Hope it's my shade," he said, and looked into her blue eyes, thinking that if he never moved from this spot, he'd be satisfied. All he could feel was the love, and that was enough. More than enough. It was everything at the moment, and he willed that moment to last forever.

"How did you sneak into here, anyway?"

"I came with the chocolate mint."

"Not an ill wind?"

"I'll ignore that. The night maid fell hard for me. She was giving out chocolate mints on all the pillows. I just kind of sweet-talked my way into my wife's room. I'm sorry," he said sincerely. "I ate the mint. I couldn't help myself. Nerves."

"This isn't funny, Alex." Cassandra moved farther into the room and looked around suspiciously for any additional surprises that might await her.

"That's precisely why I'm trying to lighten up the atmosphere. Things couldn't be a whole lot worse."

Cassandra turned slowly and faced him. "Big Charlie's dead, Alex."

Alex closed his eyes. "Yeah, I know. The big guy bought it."

"When did you know?"

Alex opened his eyes. He raked his fingers through his hair. "I heard about it last night. I called Charlie yesterday, just to tell him I was okay. One of his friends answered. They were having some kind of a meeting over at his place, a wake I guess you'd call it. Everyone was pretty drunk." Alex moved over to the window and pushed the sheer curtains aside to look out. "That leaves only the Bomb."

"And you," Cassandra said.

"And you," Alex added, turning around.

Cassandra nodded. "Tell me about it! They came after me at the airport."

"They?"

"A guy in a black suit. And another one. I could never see him. He was so fast. Wore gray and—"

Alex smiled. He had on gray slacks. He looked to the side, and she followed his gaze to the gray sweater flung on the side of the bed.

"It was you?"

"I was planning on meeting you at the airport. It wasn't like I was trying to be mysterious. I had a lot of stuff to do once I heard that Charlie was gone. I figured you'd have to take care of yourself for a few hours anyway and that you were capable. I didn't see the point in messing up your head any more than it already was with news about Charlie. I figured it would scare you if you knew I thought we'd have to make a run for it if we wanted to save our skins over the next few days. Reno seemed a good bet—lots of people and money, which means lots of cops. We could get ourselves lost for a while. Oh, I figured you'd be mad, that you might worry a little about me, but that you'd get a decent night's sleep out of the deal. Frankly, I'd do a whole lot to get a good long snooze into my own schedule. And for all I knew, your line could have been bugged. Matthison's a high flyer. He's got resources."

"Who was that man?" Cassandra asked. "The one at the airport?"

"Beats me. He could have been someone from Matthison's group. Or—hell, Cassandra, who really knows? A lot of people would have a reason to keep my engine from making it to market. At the airport, I figured I had to keep a low profile."

"The engine! Where is it?" Cassandra asked suddenly, in alarm.

"Safe and sound. I drove it out to a storage garage in Hawaiian Gardens. It's a private home, belonging to an old dude. Lives alone—cantankerous and noncommunicative as a snake with a bellyache." Alex threw her the wet washcloth. "Reminds me a lot of you."

Cassandra let the remark lie. She had other thoughts on her mind. "No one followed you?"

"Baby, it's safe. In seven days I'm pulling it out of there and driving it into the Sports Arena, disassembling it from the heap and setting it up on display."

"And what do you do for the seven days you've got left?"

"Well," he said, "I kind of thought it would be fun to..." He gave a long sideways glance at the bed.

"Sleep?" Cassandra said innocently.

"Ummm, no, I was thinking more in terms of—"

"Praying?"

"Close. The knees can enter into it..." Slowly he came closer. "And the heart," he said, holding her face in one hand. "Baby, if anything was to happen to you now." He closed his eyes tightly and stiffened his jaw to hold back an excess of emotion.

"I thought maybe you had...that maybe they had gotten to you, too," Cassandra said in a voice so soft he had to strain to hear each word. "If that had happened, I don't know what I would have done, either. I don't know how any of this got so complicated so fast. It's as if one day my life was my own and the next everything was connected to you."

He saw her face, as always beautiful, but also drawn now, and showing the signs of the exhaustion he too felt. The words she spoke held sadness. They were as much a declaration of confusion as an admission of love.

He held fast to the love, and for the time being pushed aside the more disturbing facets of their relationship. It took more bravery than facing a Brahma for him to press the issue further. "Cassandra...you just told me that you love me." She looked away, which didn't particularly surprise him. But this time he felt it was important to push past her barrier. There wasn't any guarantee of a future. There was only the present moment. He knew that, and hoped that besides understanding this intellectually, she would also accept the dire circumstances of their situation emotionally. If they were to love at all, then it had to be now. Later might never come.

"I know," she said at last in a kind of extended sigh.

He felt a sense of wild elation at her direct admission, and at the same time a sweeping sense of disappointment that her statement hadn't contained a more celebratory note to it. Love, as far as his daydreams were concerned, was supposed to be an occasion for rejoicing, which clearly, to her, it was not.

"So, what's wrong with loving me?" he asked. He had to have the answer; still, he was reluctant to hear it. But things couldn't go on as they had. The rest of the world was slipping away fast—Jerry, Charlie, possibly he, himself, would disappear next, and then all would be gone. Including this beautiful, precious woman whom he adored with his whole heart.

"Everything's wrong with it," she said forlornly. "Absolutely everything." She moved to the side of the bed and sat down on the edge. Head bent, she played with her fingers for a moment while Alex waited, knowing she understood as well as he the necessity for honesty.

At last she continued. "You aren't the man I wanted, Alex."

"No?"

"No. I wanted a man with some money, respectability, a guy who fit into a mold I had in mind."

"Ah," he said calmly, "all that." He wanted to shake her.

"Not necessarily a rich man. But a man who could at least provide some substance and security to our existence. I used to dream of a man who would sweep me off my feet, protect me from the—"

Alex stepped in and grabbed her off the bed, holding her shoulders. He hadn't expected this reaction from himself, but it had arisen so quickly there was no controlling the emotions that seemed to tear at his very core. It was as if he were reexperiencing all his father's failures again, living the pain his father may have kept hidden all of those years in addition to reeling with the agony of his own inability to be enough for the woman he loved. He wanted to strike her, wanted to shove her against the wall, and for a moment, as he gripped her shoulders, feeling the delicate framework of her body beneath his fingers, he thought he might. Instead, he pushed her roughly away.

Wild, he turned and started for the door, wanting to escape her, the room, his very self. But even if he had been dressed he still couldn't have walked away from the ravaging pain.

"I have no money now," he said. "That's true. I've never had a whole lot of anything, and what I did have usually fell apart. But I'm going to make it, baby. This time, so help me God, I'm going to make it."

Tears were streaming down her face. She was fighting her own devils and not doing a good job of it. He wanted to come to her, to slay each and every dragon at her doorstep, but he couldn't. She had to invite him in. She had to, and she had to do it now, in this one meeting, or it was never going to happen.

"Maybe, maybe, you will . . . and only if you live long enough to get that engine to the show."

"Then you take care of me. Make sure it happens."

"I have to take care of me, Alex. I don't have any engine to pull me out of my mess. I need money. Or I need that prince you aren't to come galloping up and save me from the bank. Isn't that plain? Isn't that clear? What could be more simple to understand? Just as you have everything to gain over the next few days, I have everything to lose if I continue to hang around you, dodging assassins at every corner.''

Alex was quiet. ''Okay.'' He nodded slowly. ''You're right. I've got nothing tangible to offer you right now. Right now,'' he emphasized. ''But I'd be willing to give you fifteen percent of whatever my engine brings in if you promise you'll do your best to keep me alive over the next seven days.''

''Fifteen percent? How much will fifteen percent of a dream that doesn't happen bring in?''

''It could bring in a whole lot. Or it could bring in nothing. You gotta have a dream first before you can make anything happen.''

''I've got two cats and a canary to feed, and a house to save from foreclosure. I can't bet on dreams.''

''So it's a gamble. Granted. But if you win—if we win— then you'll never have to worry about canary food again. Ralph could relax.''

''I don't know . . . I don't know what to say, Alex.''

''I love you, woman. I love you, and I want to give you everything there is on this planet, if that's what you want. But I've got to have seven days to do it.''

Cassandra chewed on her lip, shook her head several times, looked heavenward, closed her eyes, played with her fingers, sighed and finally said, ''I've always been easy prey to the old jackpot-of-life theory. I mean, it wasn't so long ago that I fell for Og's rendition of the very same tune. That taught me something, you know.''

''And that's your answer?''

''Those are the facts,'' she said. ''Of course, I've never been one to pay much attention to the facts.''

They were both very quiet, both waiting, as if for the answer to be presented by a third party.

Cassandra sighed. "Cowboy, you've got yourself a deal."

At the words, Alex gave a whoop of delight, and moving fast, lifted her into his arms. It was as if a lifetime of holding back hope and joy had suddenly been ended. Rays of invisible sunlight streamed through him. Soundless waves of laughter trilled through every cell of his body. Songs played in his heart. Oh, the long, long night of his soul's darkness had finally come to an end in one sentence, and in the embrace of this one woman.

Twirling her around, he kissed her neck, her face, her eyes, her lips. Her tears were of gladness, and tasting them was better than the finest of wines, for they brought a part of her into him. He would have all of her within him, would devour her if he could, until there was only one of them, and never, never would they ever be separate again.

The passion rose out of the joy, and slipping from his arms, Cassandra eased herself out of her clothes as he watched. He was hungry for her, wild with hunger. The desire challenged every scrap of his sensitivity. He didn't wish to wait. He wanted her now, not in ten seconds. Moving in, understanding why women called men animals, he became one. Her skirt was left on, her underwear ripped away. Already her blouse and bra were gone, or he might have torn them off, too, so enflamed was he to touch her.

With a fevered mouth, he found her lips opening to him, her tongue as demanding as his own.

"Love..." she whispered, her head thrown back as he made his way along the top curve of her breasts with mouth and hands.

Her fingers were entwined in his hair, her leg moving between his own legs until he thought he might not last long enough to feel the soft inner velvet that would draw him into ecstasy.

Her limbs were silken wands, then tapers of fire wrapped around his body as she lifted against his mouth, crying out his name, trembling in an aftermath of waning passion.

Above her, he looked into her face, and she into his. "I love you...want you..." Cassandra said, and rather than let him enter her, repositioned herself. Her body was as soft and light as a feather as she moved over him, each touch of her mouth an electric charge, every lick of her tongue bringing him to the brink of ecstasy. But he fought against his natural urge and waited, waited, until at last she moved high over him and came down slowly.

They made love that way, their eyes locked, their souls meshed, their bodies moving as one, until floating in an inner space they met completely in one shuddering, endless spasm of joy.

This was love, he thought, this was love...and there was nothing more that was needed in life. As he held Cassandra in his arms, her fair hair a starburst against his chest, he knew that he held the entire cosmos against him. Love wasn't a small compartment of life. It was life. It was all there was, and tonight, tonight...he was certain of that truth. Kissing her softly, he said her name, and in the dark of the room, she sighed in her sleep and said, "My love."

If that's what it took, then God help him, he would be this woman's prince. He would be her world, as she was his. There was something far worse than death to fear—there was the loss of love.

Chapter Seventeen

It was a magnificent morning in every way. The sun was an enormous globe, streaming dancing ribbons of light upon the earth. As the taxi sped from the hotel, Cassandra cast a longing glance out the back window. "I would have loved to have stayed."

Alex smiled and wrapped his arm more tightly around her. She felt herself melting into his eyes and knew without any question that there was no more complete feeling than this love they shared.

"We've got Hunka and Munka and Ralph to look in on," he said, still smiling.

"You really aren't angry?"

"Hey, we're family. And we'll have other times," he promised. "We'll have the best of times."

"We will," she said with equal conviction. "Oh, Alex, I do love you."

Cassandra was as happy as she had ever been, and the glow of that instant lasted during the plane ride back to Los Angeles and in the rental car they drove to her house.

They were in the small foyer of her house before the world's reality again closed in, dissolving the euphoria.

Cassandra felt it immediately upon entering the house, even before she had the concrete evidence to verify what her senses foretold. Someone had been there. While she had been away, someone had been in her house.

"What's wrong?" Alex asked, holding her back.

"Something's wrong, I don't know what. Yet." Pushing herself free, she moved into the living room, her senses acute. Alex followed behind her. She could almost feel his breath, so aware was she of her surroundings. Og had drilled her over and over again in how to be sensitive to one's environment. It was necessary to feel completely the whole world in which one lived. As all of nature was truly comprised of the same life force, one was also a part of nature, and realizing it, Og instructed, it was possible to blend oneself into any surroundings, even to remain unseen. Of course, that was for the masters of the art, and whereas Cassandra prided herself upon her acuity as a student, she was light-years away from being the perfect warrior.

But it didn't take occult powers to discern that Ralph was gone.

Halfway across the living room, Cassandra stopped in her tracks. She stared at the empty cage. Unless Ralph had developed some skills of his own, someone had let him out and nicely closed the door after him.

Cassandra pointed. Alex nodded. "Either Ralph's lost weight, or he's—"

"Gone." Rage at having the sanctity of her home violated overcame fear. Cassandra tore through the rooms, checking each one for additional signs of the intruder. Alex was with her, insisting to no avail that they hunt down the cats and get out of the house while the getting was good.

She was doing an exploration of the bathroom when she suddenly cried out, "Oh! Oh! You crazy bird!" Ralph was in the sink, fluttering about in a small amount of water. Beside him was a tiny rubber duck, something she had never owned. Ralph merely looked up at her and peeped. He was having a good time, even if she wasn't.

Alex and Cassandra exchanged looks. "I don't get it," Alex said.

"It's elementary, Watson. Someone wants me to know they can come and go as they please," she said. "Someone wants me to know that I'm watched. Someone wants me to know that they're invincible, and there's no getting away from them. Maybe they figure I'll do their dirty work for them—break you down and beg you to give them what they want so I'll be spared any more of their fun and games."

"Dangerous games," Alex said, and grabbed her elbow. "Come on, we're going to split. We're going to stay so lost over the next few days that no one, including this joker, is going to find us."

Cassandra did something out of character. She asked for help from a neighbor. She didn't like to be a bother, but old Mrs. Pritchard next door, who had lost Mr. Pritchard two years before, seemed almost honored to have Ralph as a temporary border, and said that she'd keep an eye out for Hunka and Munka, who visited her yard frequently. She wondered if they liked trout. Trout was a treat, Cassandra assured her.

As they drove, Alex glanced constantly at his rearview mirror.

"So, where are we going to hide out?" Cassandra asked glumly.

"Someplace that doesn't cost a lot."

"God, what a pair we are," Cassandra said. "Like two fugitives, drifters, no money, no place to go, no roots..."

"Very important things to you, aren't they, all that middle America stuff?"

"Suppose so," Cassandra admitted. "You know. Vine-covered castle, goldfish in the moat, flowers on the ballroom table, bird singing in the gilded cage. All of that somehow invaded my list of life's requirements."

"There's nothing wrong with that," he said.

"But it's not your thing..."

"You're my thing, baby."

"Could you be happy living like that?"

"I could give it a try." He looked over to her. "I *want* to give it a try." Alex was silent for a long while, with only occasional glances at the rearview mirror.

Cassandra studied him, wondering at the uncustomary introspection. "You're very serious," she said, by way of providing an opening for him to share his thoughts.

"Yeah. I was thinking."

"Sad thoughts?"

"Not happy ones."

"Want to talk about them?"

"Not particularly."

"Oh."

Alex sent her a glance, which softened as their eyes locked. "Okay," he said, "you want me to share. All that male sensitivity stuff."

"Not if you don't want to open up. You're entitled to your own private world."

He considered her statement, but clearing his throat, began his explanation haltingly. "I once lived in a house. A nice little house—a lot like yours. It had flowers and the smell of hot baking bread, and..." Alex cleared his throat again. "And then the flowers died and there weren't any more warm smells. I had all of that once. And when it was taken away—when it ended...I missed it a lot. I missed it so much, see, that I went far out the other way. Became a rover and a drifter, a kind of parody of the cowboy in all the cigarette commercials. Living the free life, you know."

"And?"

"And it wears thin, that kind of life. It wears thin, baby. But I just don't know anymore if I could pull the old life off again. Maybe I couldn't hack it."

"Are you afraid to try?"

"A little. But I'd do it for you," he said. "I wanted it so much, you know, and gave up ever having it. So it's a little scary opening up to the possibility again."

"Because it might not ever happen."

"Yeah. Or maybe it would happen, and like I said, maybe you can't go back again, can't pick up an old dream where it once left off. Too much other stuff's entered into your life in the interim."

"Maybe," Cassandra agreed. "But maybe you can build a new dream better than any of them."

"I'm sure as hell going to try. It's the engine, Cassandra—it's that engine that's going to make or break everything."

"The engine! Let's go see it."

"What's to see? The engine's still in the car. The car's parked in an old garage in a run-down neighborhood in a seedy part of town."

"I know, but I'd just like to see it. To make sure it still exists, kind of. To maybe talk to it, rub it, like a talisman. Please, Alex, it would make me feel better, settle my mind. So much rests on it. Everything," she said pleadingly.

"Do I have a choice?"

"No," she said, "because if you don't do what I want, I'll be like a cat on a hot tin roof the whole time."

Alex changed directions, and in forty minutes they had entered the town of Hawaiian Gardens.

"You're right," she said, "no one would think of looking here." They had come to a small pink stucco house, one in blocks of almost identical pink, beige, green and yellow stucco houses. The stucco was faded in all areas, and in others large chunks had been gouged out of the walls, as if giant creatures had taken bites.

"Nice place, huh?" Alex said.

"Charming."

"Wait till you meet the owner," he warned.

The owner came to the front door, whose screen was flapping partially out of the metal frame. Cassandra thought the man's gray pallor was due in some way to the screen's reflection, but as he stepped out onto the small concrete porch, he carried the sickly coloring with him into the bright sunlight.

"Thought I'd take a look at my car," Alex explained.

The man just looked at him, as if he had either not heard or not understood the sentence.

"So, uh, maybe you could open up the garage," Alex continued.

The man shook his head. "Car's not there."

"What do you mean the car's not there?"

The air surrounding them seemed to close in, building tension as the molecules compacted. Cassandra could almost feel her heart collapsing inward. She prayed she wasn't hearing right, even as she knew there was no mistake.

"Just what I said. Your car's gone. Someone musta hauled it off when I was gone or sleepin'. 'Cause it's not here now. Figured you musta come t'get it."

"I want to see," Alex demanded, setting off on his own down the driveway in the direction of the attached garage.

The man shrugged and slopped along behind them. Alex looked down at the broken lock, dangling from the hinge. He raised the garage door, and they all stared into an empty expanse.

"Alex..." Cassandra said, her fingers holding fast to his arm, which hung limp at his side. All strength, even his usually robust coloring, seemed to have evaporated from his being. "Alex, there's got to be some explanation—"

"Sure," he said, whirling on his heel and striding off down the driveway. "The bastards just beat us."

"You owe me for the broke lock," the man called after them as Cassandra ran to catch up with Alex. He had already climbed into the front seat of the rental car.

The man clamored after them. "You owe me for the lock!"

Cassandra swung around, her hands on the car's door handle. "You've lost a lock? This man's lost an entire life!"

"It's five bucks you owe me."

"So bill me," she said, and slammed the door.

Alex was calm, too calm as he drove down the freeway again toward Los Angeles. Neither of them spoke. What was there to say? Platitudes were of no use anymore. The sun simply wasn't going to come up tomorrow. There was no silver lining to the darkest cloud. One couldn't even whistle a happy tune. Certainly, as the song went, they had walked through the storm with their heads held high, even though they had been afraid of the dark, but now the worst had happened, and they were plain out of inspiration.

When they came to the Santa Monica Freeway interchange, Cassandra finally spoke. "You're taking me home?"

"Yeah. You'll be safe now. They've got what they wanted."

She should have been relieved, but she wasn't. "And you?"

"I'll just be what I was before. A rover and a drifter, a cowboy legend."

"You can't rope steers anymore. Your rodeo days have ended. What are you going to do, Alex?"

"Baby," he said, not turning to look at her, "what the hell difference does it make to you?"

"What?" she asked, feeling his words like a slap across her face.

"Cassandra, Cassandra...you made it all too clear. Your ideas of castles and men on white horses—I can't give you that. I can't give you anything. So just let it be, okay? Don't make things any worse, any more difficult for either of us than they are already. We'd have maybe a month of something that could be called 'trying,' and after that, it would be—"

"Be what?" Cassandra asked. She had listened to each word, but behind the statements, which certainly made sense on one level, there was another stratum of feeling he was keeping to himself.

"It would be the way it was when the flowers stopped blooming in our yard. It would be the way it was when there were no more pies in the oven. On the wall, see, there would be this invisible sign where Home Sweet Home used to hang. Once, it used to hang there. One day that was gone, too. That sign, which everyone knew was there, in spite of it being invisible, had one word on it: Failure."

His face was contorted into bitterness, and she could imagine him as he once was, a young boy with wide gray eyes, a slight frame, stricken with disappointment after disappointment, standing in that barren landscape that had once been a blooming garden.

She moved closer and put her arms around him. "It doesn't have to be like that, Alex."

He shrugged her off with a twist of his shoulders. "Let it be, Cassandra!"

The words were like the snap of a whip. He meant it. He really meant to end it.

In front of her house, he kept the engine idling as he waited for her to get out.

She didn't. Instead, she sat in place, staring out the window, wanting him to say something to make everything all right again, and knowing that he wasn't going to make the gesture to save the relationship. She couldn't reach him now, no matter what she said. His enemies were in the past, and that was where he had gone. In his pain, she hardly existed for him. With the old pain, he was in familiar territory. He knew the depth and breadth and degree of that misery. To add her to his burden would be something unbearable. After waiting for as long as she could, she slipped out of the car and closed the door. He drove away before she had entered her house. Glancing back, she watched the car speed out of her life.

And that is how men on white horses leave, she thought. Never had she imagined the leaving. She always saw them arriving. And men on white horses were supposed to stay. Everyone knew that. Except Alex.

Chapter Eighteen

How can someone be in your life one hundred percent and then not exist anymore? How can a person fill you with their love until every ounce of doubt has been squeezed out and then withdraw the feeling, leaving you an empty shell?

Cassandra stood in front of Ralph's cage, staring into his tiny mirror. Ralph hopped onto his swing. Tiny bells attached to the small wooden perch jingled.

"You don't have any answers for me, do you, fella?"

Cocking his head at her, Ralph chirped some unknown message. Those were the only sounds in the house.

Hunka was curled on the sofa, where a beam of light from the window behind collected in a soft, diffused pool on the light blue velvet. Munka lay snoozing before the fireplace. A paper log, bought from the grocery store, gave off leaping flames of blue and yellow.

Cassandra had thought solace might be found in the quiet, homey atmosphere she had purposely created. All of this was supposed to mean something. It was supposed to prove something. This was what she had manufactured for herself, by herself, in that time when she was waiting for her prince to show up.

Well, he had come and left. That was something she hadn't counted on, not in any of her scenarios.

The buzzer went off in the kitchen, and she abandoned the domestic scene to check on the brownies she had baked for Mrs. Pritchard as thanks for watching the cats and Ralph.

Like her relationship with Alex, all of what was around her appeared so solid and continuing. But in a matter of days the bank would send her another official notice. She would be ordered to clear out. The fire would burn no more. The oven would cease to be warm. There would be no blue velveteen fabric beneath the window to catch the winter sunlight.

One day someone else would move into her house. She didn't know if that made her glad or sad. A little of both, she finally decided, as she carefully set the brownies on a trivet to cool.

Returning to the living room, she picked up the classified section of the newspaper again, where she had been circling possible job opportunities. But her mind couldn't stay on the fine print, and tears dropped one after the other on the paper, making the print blur. She supposed she cried herself to sleep. When she awoke, it was almost dark in the house, and chilly. The fire had all but burned itself out. Only the tiniest glow was left, a faint ball of red ember amid ashes, like a dying heart, she thought.

The sudden rap on her door made her own heart leap. In the silence it made a thunderous racket, rousing instantaneous fear. But she didn't know if she had it left in her to resist any more trouble. What was the use?

"Cassandra! Cassandra!"

That it was Alex's voice seemed so unlikely she could only remain transfixed in the chair, waiting for the haunting to dissolve. In twilight, the room's atmosphere contained a curious fuzziness to it. She thought it would be possible to stroke the air as if it were a piece of linty flannel. The conscious state bled into a world of dreams. The voice couldn't be real.

"Cassandra?"

The pounding continued. It was him...it was Alex at her door.

"I got six egg rolls," he said when they faced each other in the open door. He was carrying a large brown bag. "I wasn't sure if you liked the hot stuff or not, so I took the liberty of getting a pretty wide selection."

"Why are you back here?" she asked.

He met her gaze steadily. "I was in the neighborhood."

"Go away, leave me alone, let me have some peace."

"I thought you liked Chinese food."

His gray eyes were pouring out more emotion than she could hold inside. There wasn't room in her for the two of them. She tried to close the door, but he stepped forward, wedging his foot in the jamb.

"I don't have a kingdom to lay at your feet," he said. "Chinese is all I can offer you."

"It hurt, Alex. That hurt, you walking out on me like that."

"I know." He looked miserable, as rotten as she felt. "Look, see..." He tipped the bag toward her. "I brought more than hors d'oevres, if that means anything."

"I'd just like it to end, okay? No jokes, no egg rolls. Especially no more pain."

"Hey, it wasn't a whole barrel of laughs for me either, kid." His eyes were clouded over with a moist film. He swallowed and looked off to the side. "This is highly embarrassing. In movies, cowboys don't do this sort of thing." He wiped at his eyes with his sleeve. Looking into the bag, he said, "So, uh, I got two kinds of rice—fried and white. Didn't want to blow it, you know. Big chance here...last chance...I love you," he said, his eyes fixed to the top of a plain white container. "Woman, I can't live without you." Then he dared look up.

Cassandra was crying. Hunka's tail was winding around her leg, and Munka was staring up with interest at the bag. Sniffing, she rubbed the back of her hand against her cheek, staying a tear. "I feel trapped. By you. By me. I don't know what to say."

"Just say you like chop suey."

"What should I do?" she asked the universe.

Alex's expression was riddled with every ounce of pain she was feeling. "Invite me in," he said urgently.

"Just so you can leave me again?"

"I won't, I won't. Besides, the egg rolls are getting cold. Please, baby..."

"I mean it, Alex. If you step over this threshold it's—"

"Forever. Forever, okay?"

Cassandra sighed. "I like wontons. You got any wontons?"

"Yeah," he said, and smiled. "I got wontons."

She stepped aside, allowing him to take the journey back into her life.

They were two people with nothing but each other. Giddy with misery, they became reckless seekers of every sort of free hedonistic activity available within an hour's drive. Every meal was relished with a kind of celebratory exhilaration, tinged with the somberness of a last supper presented to the condemned. They made love frequently and creatively, once even on the beach in a secluded cove where the water crested a stone's throw away and the salt spray dampened their blanket. There were walks along the Venice boardwalk, where they bought ice creams and gave quarters to panhandlers playing guitars out of tune.

Alex tried to call the Bomb at his restaurant three or four times, but each time was told Gordo was out. It worried Alex when he couldn't get hold of him. He wanted to let Gordo know about the theft of the engine. Knowing the Bomb, Alex said, he'd be out shooting off his mouth a mile a minute now about how they were going to be rich and famous. Alex wanted to spare Gordo that kind of humiliation. The disappointment was something he'd have to handle his own way.

"How long before the balloon bursts?" Alex asked after three days of being together. They were in the market getting cat food.

Cassandra shrugged. "Could be a week, two weeks, tomorrow."

"And then?"

"And then I'm out of paradise, back into the cold cruel world of evil landlords."

"The automotive show's in three days," he said.

"Don't think about it." Cassandra threw a couple of cans of cat food into her shopping cart.

"No, I want to go," he said. "Really."

"Turn up the vegetable aisle. You're crazy."

"Of course. And I want you to come, too."

"Look, Alex, you know I'd follow you through hell—I already have—but I don't see the point in twisting the knife, you know? I mean it's over and done with. The engine's gone. The dreams are gone—yours and mine. Finished, over, kaput. Between us, we've got zilcho. Grab that small can of creamed corn."

"I would have won," he said stubbornly, reaching for the corn. "I only want to see the competition. I want to know I would have won, that it wasn't just some delusion." He stopped wheeling the shopping cart. "Please," he said. "I'd really like us to go. Together."

"I'm not going to dress up for this funeral," Cassandra said emphatically.

"I love you," Alex said just as emphatically, sweeping her into his arms.

On the first day of the automotive show, they were among the first to enter the Sports Arena. The parking lot was filling up rapidly. There had been a lot of publicity over the show, with its promise of futuristic revelations. Not only the car buffs, but the computer hackers and science fiction nuts were out in full force.

The contest judging the inventions would be held later in the afternoon. Alex had wanted time to peruse the competition at his leisure.

"Maybe you could do it again?" Cassandra said as they wandered up and down aisles where manufacturers and

specialty vendors hawked their wares in elaborately decorated booths. America was the Mecca of the automobile
business, and Los Angeles was the city where people didn't
use their feet except to kick tires. No expense was spared
on the displays.

"Uh-uh," Alex said wearily. "That was it. It took
everything out of me. I'll find something, but I'm through
climbing mountains. Falling down hurts too much."

"What do you think?" Cassandra asked, now that they
had cruised the exhibits for more than two hours. She
couldn't tell if Alex was elated or depressed.

"I would have taken it," he said. "The world would
have been mine. Detroit would have groveled at my
boots."

"Would you settle for some popcorn?" She jerked her
head at a vendor nearby.

He stepped in front of her and held her by the shoulders as he looked into her face. "Cassandra, I wanted to
give you so much. I wanted to save your house. I wanted
to make you proud."

She shook her head. "Look," she said, staring down at
her toes, "it's like this: I'm wearing a lot of makeup. If I
cry, it's going to be a very bad scene. I'm going to be a
dead ringer for the Phantom of the Opera. Black streaky
holes for eyes. I can't make any kind of serious speeches,
Alex, or I'm going to fall apart. You've just got to know,
by now, that I love you." She managed to meet his eyes. "I
would have liked that—you coming up with the dough to
rescue the bird and the cats and the damsel in distress. I
won't tell you I wouldn't have been thrilled to the bottom
of my hope chest. But—and I never thought I'd say this—
somehow when you love someone, and know that he loves

you, too, everything else seems semi-incidental. I'll survive.''

Alex got the popcorn. It came in a big cardboard barrel, the giant size. Their feet needed a break, and Cassandra led the way to the show's central decorative feature, a giant free-form modernistic metal sculpture. The display was dramatically positioned on a float in the middle of a large pool of water. Cassandra and Alex took places on the low ledge surrounding it. Behind them, a cascading stream of water gushed over the sculpture, creating an interesting waterfall effect.

The scene around them was electric with excitement. In the two hours since they had arrived, crowds had invaded the spacious area. It was a fun show, a hopeful show, and voices rang with gleeful admiration and surprise at the products displayed. The entries in the futuristic contest were arranged in one long row, almost a concourse, really. The area had a wide crimson carpet running its length, as if to herald the kings of the future. From where they sat it was possible to view the delighted expressions of the inventors and visitors alike. The fountain behind them gurgled pleasantly over the metal rods.

"Let's move," Cassandra said, noting the saddened expression on Alex's face. "In fact," she said, jumping up with the half-empty popcorn barrel, "let's go home right now and make love for the next eight hours!" Clowning, she raised her eyes and let them travel languorously downward, but along the way she stopped and gasped. "Alex—" She took a step forward, her attention transfixed on something behind him.

Alex turned, saw nothing but the fountain, then turned back, the unbelievable occurring to him.

Cassandra stood stock-still. Pointing at the fountain, she asked weakly, "Alex...Alex...what if that were...?

Alex looked. It took more than a few long looks to be sure—to make him accept the vision before him.

There, hidden behind a wall of flowing water, and augmented by various rods sticking out at odd dramatic angles, was his engine, camouflaged as a metal sculpture.

Chapter Nineteen

It took a lot of fast talking, but between the two of them they were able to convince the contest's governing committee of their situation.

"This sounds crazy," one of the men said. Actually, several of them said it.

"Yes. It is crazy," Alex replied. But he pointed out that, crazy as everything certainly was, it didn't alter the fact that the show's main decorative arrangement was none other than his stolen engine tarted up a bit with rods and doodads and a lot of flowing water.

In the end the committee gave into his raving and allowed him to reenter the contest as long as the display was in place by four that afternoon.

Cassandra enlisted any able-bodied man she could flirt with into helping dismantle the engine from the fountain.

Alex got permission to use a back storage area for his reassembling.

"I don't know what all this stuff is," Cassandra complained. Before her were tools of every conceivable size and shape, borrowed—after more clever pleading—from the displays of various automotive tool vendors on the premises.

"Okay, okay, just hand me the thing that looks like a lizard with his tongue cut out."

"They all look that way. I'd like to see you bake a cake."

And so it went, feverish work and harsh words.

The dark shadow fell over Cassandra when she was trying to locate a wrench that, according to Alex, looked like a monkey.

At first she thought the single light overhead had dimmed. "Damn..." she said, looking up. But instead of a light, she saw the face of a man staring down at her. Slightly behind him were two other men. None of them looked particularly friendly. Cassandra cleared her throat. "Uh, Alex..."

Alex looked up. His expression changed from bewilderment to surprise to joy. "Hey *paisano*!" he said, rising from the floor.

"Alex, he has a gun," Cassandra said faintly.

The flush of happy surprise faded from Alex's face; it changed to knowledgeable disgust.

"Hey, you think I like this?" Gordo "the Bomb" Bombolina waved his gun expressively.

"Do me a favor, Gordo, just this once, don't talk with your hands, okay?"

"Yeah, sorry."

"You're sorry? I don't know what to think here." Alex shook his head. "I mean, this can't be happening."

"Yeah," Gordo said, "it's like Caesar, huh? *Et tu*."

"Don't give yourself credit. Brutus you ain't."

"My own name's going to mean something now, Alex."

"Son of a bitch, Gordo..." Alex made a move toward him but was stopped short by the cocking of Gordo's gun. "Oh, great. Nice touch. Even a silencer, huh? Just like the big, bad boys."

Cassandra couldn't believe this was the man she had imagined. The Bomb's voice was raspy and rather thin for being such a heavy man. He seemed a person in the wrong body, in the wrong business. What she felt was apparently not that far off course, she figured, as Gordo went on to plead his own case.

"I didn't want to do this, Rocky. I mean, it started out just the way it was. Investing in your engine. But then things got kind of cockeyed, and I didn't see no way out of the mess I got into."

"What mess is that?" Alex asked disgustedly.

Cassandra hoped Alex wouldn't do anything silly, like try to rescue them. As for herself, she was gauging the gun's distance from where she stood, with an eye toward knocking it out of his hand. She was certain she could deck the Bomb in nothing flat. But she didn't know about his two friends. They might have weapons of their own.

"Well," the Bomb said, obviously shamed, "I shot my mouth off a little. The guys from the neighborhood—you know how it is. They came in, and they're talking like always about their big deals this and their big deals that. So I'm only human, right? I let go with a little of my own. One thing led to another, as they say, and I'm invited in again. They're seeing their way clear to giving me another chance. All I had to do was see that the engine didn't get to market. It's going to screw things up for some boys in Detroit.''

"You're here to kill me."

"Yeah, and I want you to know, Rock, I don't like it one little bit. I told them as much. But it's a club. You gotta keep the rules. You know them guys, Rocky. You play ball their way or not at all. They're very strict that way.''

"And Matthison? He was part of your group?" Alex asked.

"Him!" Gordo said with a snarl. "That snake. He came from somewhere up above. I don't know where. He works with the top of the top, where they don't use no names even.''

"So, besides having to do me in, you had to get the others, too.''

"You even killed poor Jerry," Cassandra accused.

The Bomb appeared affronted. "No," he said, "No, not Jerry. Oh, I took credit for it with the boys, of course. It was a bit of luck, that fall. For me—not for Jerry. But I had nothing to do with him falling down the stairs. He must have tripped. He'd gotten so nuts, thinking of how he was going to be a rich man and all. I think he just lost control of his muscles, all that jittering around he was doing. Or," Gordo said darkly, "it could have been Doris. Doris hated him. And you know as well as I do she's meaner than a nest of scorpions.''

"What about Charlie?" Alex demanded.

"Oh, oh...Charlie." Gordo shook his head sadly. "I always warned him. Would he ever listen? No, not ever. Always with the extra cheese, the little more of this sauce, a spicy something here, a sweet too many there. He ate like a pig, Alex. You know that. We all knew that. Charlie died of piggishness, plain and simple.''

"But you took credit?" Cassandra said.

Gordo shrugged, extending his hands and lowering his gun for just a moment. "Why not? It gave me a little glory. What's the harm? Would the truth have brought back Charlie?"

"But you could have warned Alex. You could have tried to save him—and me—from Matthison."

"Ah, yes. And I thought about it, too. Don't think I didn't think about it. But it was really out of my hands by then. Matthison's very smart. He's like a machine. You start it, it doesn't shut off. I was helpless, Rocky. Nothing I could do by that point but to go along. So here I am." Gordo heaved his shoulders, sighing. He looked sadly at Alex. Little beads of sweat began to break out on his forehead, and a flush filled his heavy cheeks. "I've never carried through on one lousy crime," Gordo said. "I'm sorry. If I'm going to make anything of myself, you're my last chance, Alex."

"If it's the money..." Cassandra pleaded.

"Forget it, Cassandra," Alex said sadly. "This hasn't got a thing to do with money."

"No, no," Gordo replied. "Money isn't the issue here. It's honor. Look, please, try to understand my position. This is in no way personal, me having to kill you. And, miss, I like women, really I do. And, Alex, you know how I've always felt about you...we're like the closest. But I've got to do it. For the honor." He leveled the gun, and with painful slowness, his hand trembling wildly, brought his third finger forward, a hair from the trigger. "This isn't easy, not at all."

"No!" Cassandra leaped forward, kicking the gun out of Gordo's hand.

At the same time, a terrible sound overrode her own voice. *"Aii-hiii."* The wail came out of nowhere. Suddenly two other guns were flying through the air, and Gordo Bombolina was scraping the concrete with his nose as the other two men were being simultaneously bashed against opposite walls, like pool balls split by an expert's shot.

Cassandra gasped. "My God, you!"

Ogata Kenzo smiled and did a tricky and extraneous kick for her, accompanied by an "Aii-haii-yaii!"

"Such a show-off," she said, shaking her head.

"Shogun! Modern style," he corrected. Dressed entirely in black, Ogata Kenzo executed one last fluid movement, then picked up the guns, removed the bullets and dropped all three weapons onto Gordo's splayed fingers.

"There is no honor in these things," Og lamented dramatically. "Honor is in here," he went on, pointing to his own insides. "Honor is in the soul."

"Give me a break," moaned Cassandra.

Og shrugged and grinned. "Well, that's what all the books say. How you guys doin'?"

Og had read in the paper about Jerry's death. To be honest, he explained to Cassandra and Alex—even to the three hapless thugs—he had felt a little personal responsibility for the misfortune. He had started to worry about Cassandra, fearing she might be stupid enough to be honorable and try to pay off his own dishonor by good deeds.

So now and again, he had kept his eye on her. The more he had kept an eye on her, the more his conscience had bothered him, and he had become certain something very nasty was going down. Of course, as he explained to both Cassandra and Alex, he had dared not show his face around town, seeing as how he was a marked man himself—what with the host of angry creditors ready to chomp on his heels. But he had kept tabs on Cassandra and Alex anyway, just out of good sportsmanship.

"You were at my shack," Alex said, certain of himself. "It was you who put out the fire."

Og snickered with glee. "I really spoiled their day."

But the Matthison event had really worried him, and had Alex not handled that matter himself, well...he had been reluctantly prepared to don a ninja outfit and do some kind of spectacular Bruce Lee number out there.

"Did you know Matthison's guys followed you out to Hawaiian Gardens?" Og asked Alex. "Of course you didn't know." Og shook his head, then grinned. "I knew. I was there, too. The whole way, baby..."

Og figured he had probably beaten them by minutes the day he had removed the engine.

"I figured the best way to keep the engine safe was to do something oriental. I convinced the show's promoters I was the hottest new artist in town. Og the Great can do anything," he said, winking. "So I rendered it invisible— the first ninja engine—by putting it directly into view. But with a twist. A lot of rods and water. Anyway, people hardly ever really see what they're looking at. I was going to have the whole thing set up for you by the time of the judging. A surprise."

By this time, Cassandra felt she was going to faint. "Og, I just can't take any more...of anything."

"Yeah," he agreed, "I know what you mean. But all's well that ends well," he said, and kicked Gordo in the rump as he attempted to rise.

"That was you in my house, too?"

"I was leaving you clues."

"You were making me crazy."

"I wanted you out of there. You should be more care-ful, Cassandra. You're too trusting." Og moved over to where the two men were slumped against the walls, and one at a time, pressed his fingers against the backs of their ears. Out like lights, they slithered to the floor. "Old ninja trick," he said with a chuckle. "Love that showy stuff, just love it..."

"I'd never realized you were so concerned over the wel-fare of others," Alex said, and Cassandra could tell from his voice, if not his expression, that Og had already made his mark. Alex was impressed, God help him.

"Well," Og said, "I figured that any engine that was worth all that interest must be worth a great deal of money. Any man who can stay alive to get that money is going to be smart enough to want to invest it. And I'm a man who happens to have a few good ideas..." His smile conveyed a million schemes.

Shortly after six o'clock that evening, the judges tallied up their responses to the inventions submitted for consid-eration. It was unanimous. The cowboy took the day.

Three days later Alex, dressed in a new suit, returned to Santa Monica, carrying an attaché case.

"Howdy, ma'am," he said, standing at the door. "Just rode in from Detroit. Got a powerful thirst. Got an even more powerful hankering for a woman."

"So, what do you want first?"

"First, last, and always, I'll take the filly."

Cassandra was half undressed when she saw the pile of green bills on the bed. Alex was lounging on his side, watching her. He wore his crooked, self-satisfied grin—much like Og's, Cassandra thought.

"What's all that?" she asked.

"Your fifteen percent for keeping me alive," he informed.

"You're kidding?"

"A deal's a deal. I made it, babe. I really made it. The good guys in Detroit bought my engine rather than have it go to some of the bad guys in other countries. Also, I signed a deal with an industrial think tank, where they pay me a lot of hay every month just to conjure up ideas...and I'm already conjuring."

Cassandra sank down on the bed and began to count the money. When she got to fifty thousand she stopped. "This is too much, Alex. This will pay off the loan on our house, and we can—" She stopped suddenly, something in his face frightening her. "What's wrong?"

"Our house?"

"Our house. Yes."

"Your house."

Cassandra stared at him, the message he was stating so obtusely becoming clear. "I thought that you loved me. I mean, that was kind of very, very clear, Alex. There was a lot of talk...Chinese food...things we said in bed...out of bed..."

"I do love you."

"Then..."

Alex grabbed her hands and held them together. The money she had been holding fell like leaves from her fingers and fluttered to the mattress. They were attached physically, yet he couldn't meet her eyes. She stared down at his head. It was bent, weighted by suffering she supposed, but at the moment she didn't much care. She was filling up to the brim with that old pain he had brought to her on more than one occasion—and had promised her he would never inflict upon her again.

"Cassandra, I love you, I do," he muttered in a strained voice. "But, babe, I'm not the marrying kind of guy. Maybe after a while. Someday. When I said love, it meant love...but not, you know. I was thinking, anyway, that we could maybe try out this relationship on a semipermanent basis—"

"You mean live together?"

"Yes," he said, finally raising his eyes.

"No."

"I thought you loved me?" he countered.

"Yeah," she said bitterly, shaking inside so hard she could hardly form thoughts that made any sense. "But see, Alex, I'm just not your basic live-in kind of a gal. My game's commitment. As in all or nothing, Alex."

"I can't do that," he said quietly. And in his voice, as well as his face, Cassandra knew that was the way it was. He really couldn't bring himself to make that final step in the relationship. How could she have been so stupid? She assumed he wanted exactly what she wanted.

"I'll take my fifteen percent," Cassandra said with a dullness that belied her inner state. "I figure I earned it."

"Cassandra..."

"I'm going in there to take a bath. When I get out of it, I want you gone. Out of this house and out of my life. No more Chinese food at the door. I've lost my appetite for Chinese food. And cowboys. Just so you know..."

When she came out, he was gone.

She had meant what she had said about not being a live-in kind of a woman. That truly was the way it was, just as for Alex being a drifter and loner, besides being a lover, was his way. Nevertheless, if he had shown up at her door with some Chinese food, she would probably be glad to see an egg roll.

She missed him. And she loved him like crazy.

But it was over and done with. Even after a month.

It was hard to get on with her life again. Og was back wheeling and dealing like mad. When he found out she had gotten money from Alex, he nearly went crazy. With all the publicity from the engine deal, he was receiving offers to become a screen idol in the image of Bruce Lee. The cops had made it seem as if he had single-handedly broken up the top guns of a Mafia family. The Bomb had looked ecstatic in all the news pictures. He had finally made it.

She hated herself, but Og finally wore her down, and she agreed to be his production manager in a film he'd talked an independent movie company into financing. It was called *Dragon Eater*. They were supposed to start filming in three weeks. She was even promised a fat salary.

Meanwhile, she had time to paint a couple of her rooms and get some plumbing work done. The rest of the time she spent licking her wounds.

She was high on a ladder, dripping paint onto her hair as she put the finishing touches on a corner of her bedroom ceiling, when the doorbell rang. She thought of letting it go, but when the visitor insisted on pounding, indignation brought her striding to the door.

It was Alex. It was a shock. She was truly surprised to see him. Although she had thought of him day and night since they had last been together, this was one of the times when her mind had just drifted off course. She could only stare dumbly at his form, looming on the other side of the front portal.

"Don't worry," he said without much inflection. "I'm not bearing Chinese food."

He was dressed in slick cowboy duds, including boots and a hat. Instead of looking silly in the city, he looked wonderful—sexy and masculine as hell. The best-looking rover and drifter the women in Los Angeles were ever going to set eyes upon, Cassandra thought ruefully.

"It's okay. I'm not hungry." She waited to hear why he had come.

"I was just off to Vegas," he said, "but they delivered your car. At last. Figured I'd drop it by on my way out."

"Oh..." She looked beyond him. There it was, her old Fiat, parked at the curb. "I figured I'd have to tell the insurance agency."

"It's in good running order."

"It looks wonderful," she said honestly. "It's got new paint, too. Thanks." She stared up at him, wishing for some sign that he wanted to make amends. Somehow it had to come from him. Maybe...maybe she loved him enough to bend her rules a little, but at this point he had to make some major effort to let her know she was truly important to him.

He didn't. In the next breath he said, "So, the point is, I've got to take off for the airport right away, and I'm either going to have to call a cab from here or prevail upon you to drop me off in the Fiat."

"Okay, sure" she said instantly, hiding her feelings. "I can take you." Then she remembered her appearance. "Oh," she said, looking down. "It'll just take a minute to change."

"I'll wait out here," he said.

And then she knew absolutely: it was over, entirely finished between them.

They drove to the airport practically in silence. Now and then they made small talk. Alex said he'd been working on this new idea for another engine and was off to talk to some investors about it.

"Sound's great," she said, feeling left out. Before she had been an integral part of his deals, of his life. Now she was a taxi driver.

At the airport she slowed to a stop at the curb. He thanked her and grabbed his luggage from the car. "God...Oh..." he groaned. "Shoulder...damn."

Cassandra was around by his side at once. "Here," she said, "let me."

"Thanks. Don't know...maybe I'll have to have it operated on."

"Maybe," Cassandra said, lifting the bag. "This doesn't seem that heavy, either."

"Probably just the way I lifted it. Think you might carry it up to the check-in counter for me?"

She didn't mind at all. If she had her way, she would have made this final meeting between them last forever and a day.

As they approached the counter, Alex said, "You know Vegas—they've got all that money, and all those people, and the cops."

"Yeah," Cassandra said, remembering the time they had spent there together. Life may have been scary then, but it sure was beautiful, too. "I remember."

"What a place," Alex said, shaking his head. "They've got everything. Even got places to get married at the drop of a hat—if someone feels they'd like to do something dumb like that."

Alex stopped. And the hat suddenly fell between them, landing half on Alex's boot, half on her shoe.

Cassandra stared down at it, then looked back up at Alex. "You dropped your hat," she said cautiously.

"Yup. Sure did." He was waiting, the tension in his face matching what she was feeling.

"What would it mean if I were to pick up that hat?"

"That I've got a use for this extra ticket in my hand." He fanned out two commuter tickets to Las Vegas.

Slowly, her eyes never leaving his, she began to bend down. But not alone. Alex joined her, and together they brought the hat back up.

"Nice hat," she said with tears in her eyes. She placed it on his head, giving it a slight tug over his forehead.

"I'm back," he said. "I'm back, Cassandra...to stay forever if you'll have me forever." He kissed her hard then, harder than she had ever imagined it was possible to be kissed, as if he were afraid she might drift away. But that was impossible. She was bound to him forever by love.

"Well," she said when she had caught her breath, "I guess this is it then."

"Looks that way. The whole gig...till death do us part."

"Alex, uh, I'd appreciate it if you wouldn't say it quite that way..."

He smiled. It was that wonderful, crooked smile, the same one he had smiled on the day they had met.

* * * * *

Silhouette Special Edition

COMING NEXT MONTH

#409 A CERTAIN SMILE—Lynda Trent
Impulsive widow Megan Wayne and divorced father Reid Spencer didn't have marriage in mind, but what harm could come if their friendship turned into something stronger? Reid's two teenage daughters didn't intend to let them find out....

#410 FINAL VERDICT—Pat Warren
Prosecutor Tony Adams's upbringing had built him a strong case against lasting love. Could attorney Sheila North's evidence to the contrary weaken his defenses and free his emotions from solitary confinement?

#411 THUNDERSTRUCK—Pamela Toth
Crew member Honey Collingsworth accepted the risks of hydroplane racing. Still, when her brother and dashing defector Alex Checkhov competed, churning up old hatred, she feared for their lives...and her heart.

#412 RUN AWAY HOME—Marianne Shock
Proud landowner Burke Julienne knew that to restless vagabond Savannah Jones, the lush Julienne estate was just another truck stop. Yet he found her mesmerizing, and he prayed that one day Savannah would trade freedom for love.

#413 A NATURAL WOMAN—Caitlin Cross
When farmer's daughter Vana Linnier abruptly became a sophisticated celebrity, she desperately needed some plain old-fashioned horse sense to cope with her jealous sister and her disapproving but desirable boss, Sky Van Dusen.

#414 BELONGING—Dixie Browning
Saxon Evanshaw returned home to a host of family fiascos and the lovely but stealthy estate manager, Gale Chandler. Who was she really? Where were the missing family treasures? And would Gale's beauty rob him of his senses?

AVAILABLE THIS MONTH:

Starting in October...

SHADOWS ON THE NILE

by

Heather Graham Pozzessere

A romantic short story in six installments from best-selling author Heather Graham Pozzessere.

The first chapter of this intriguing romance will appear in all Silhouette titles published in October. The remaining five chapters will appear, one per month, in Silhouette Intimate Moments' titles for November through March '88.

Don't miss *"Shadows on the Nile"*—a special treat, coming to you in October. Only from Silhouette Books.

Be There!

IMSS-1